John Lydgate, Charles Edward TAME

The life of our Lady Part I.

With glossary and a biographical notice of the author

John Lydgate, Charles Edward TAME

The life of our Lady Part I.
With glossary and a biographical notice of the author

ISBN/EAN: 9783741164996

Manufactured in Europe, USA, Canada, Australia, Japa

Cover: Foto ©Raphael Reischuk / pixelio.de

Manufactured and distributed by brebook publishing software
(www.brebook.com)

John Lydgate, Charles Edward TAME

The life of our Lady Part I.

The Life of Our Lady.

THE

Life of Our Lady.

PART I.

EDITED FROM MSS. IN THE BRITISH MUSEUM

BY

CHARLES EDWARD TAME,

AUTHOR OF "THE SUPREMACY OF THE HOLY SEE,"
"THE CHURCH'S LAW," ETC.

With Glossary and a Biographical Notice of the Author.

London:

R. WASHBOURNE, 18, PATERNOSTER ROW.

Sancte et Indibidue Trinitati
Jesu Cristi crucifixi bumanitati gloriose beate Marie Virgini
sit sempiterna gloria
ab omnia creatura
per infinita seculorum secula.
Amen.

BIOGRAPHICAL NOTICE.

" Chaucer, floure of rethoryke eloquence,
Compyled bookes plesaunt and mervayllous ;
After hym noble Gower, experte in scynce,
Wrote moralytees harde and delycyous ;
But Lydgates workes are fruyteful and sentencyous,
Who of his bookes hathe redde the fyne
He wyll hym cal a famous rethorycyne."
      Prologue, FEYLDIS *Controversye betusne a Lover and a Jaye.*

" O mayster Lydgate, the most dulcet sprynge
Of famous rethoryke, wyth balade ryall
The chefe orygynal."
                STEPHEN HAWES, *Pastyme of Pleasure.*

AN JOHN LYDGATE, the accomplished author of
the " Life of Our Lady," the " Story of Thebes,"
the " History of Troy," and upwards of 250 miscel-
laneous pieces and ditties, was, as he himself tells
us, " borne in Lydegate " (Harl. MS. 2251, fol. 283), a small village
in the county of Suffolk, a few miles from St. Edmundsbury,
but in what year this event took place our author omits to tell
us. We may, however, with the assistance of the registers
containing the entries of the dates of his consecration to the
successive orders in the Church, arrive at a satisfactory solu-
tion of the doubt as to the time of his birth, which we may with
certainty place in the year 1368, or thirty-two years before the
death of " my master Chaucer," as Lydgate calls him. There
is extant a very remarkable autobiographical tract of Lidgate,
entitled his " Testament," which, while giving a very graphic

description of the author's childhood, is evidently a faithful index of the time in which Lydgate lived. Our extracts are from the Harl. MS. 2255, fol. 47—66, a very fair MS.; other copies are Harl. MS. 218; Jes. Coll. Camb. MS. Q Γ 8; Bib. Reg. MS. 18 D 11, a later copy. From this "Testament" it does not appear that Lydgate while a child showed any signs of precocity, or of that brilliant genius which afterward developed in him. He describes himself at this period as being—

> Voyde of resoun ; yove to wilfulnesse ;   81
> Froward to vertu ; of thrift gafe litil heede ;
> Loth to lerne ; lovid no besynesse
> Sauf play or merthe ; straunge to spelle or reede ;
> Folwyng al appetites, longyng to childheede ;
> Lihtly tournyng, wylde and seelde sadde,
> Weepyng for nouhte, and anoon offtir glad.

> For litil wroth to stryve with my felawe   82
> As my passiouns did my bridil leede ;
> Of the yeerde somtyme I stood in awe,
> To be scooryd, that was al my dreede,—
> Loth toward scole, lost my tyme indeede ;
> Lik a yong colt that ran withoute brydil
> Made my freendys ther good to spende in ydil.

> I hadde in custome to come to scole late,   83
> Nat for to lerne, but for a contenaunce ;
> With my felawys reedy to debate ;
> To jangle and jape was set al my plesaunce,
> Wherof rebukyd this was my chevisaunce,
> To forge a lesyng and therupon to muse,
> Whan I trespassid mysilven to excuse.

> To my bettre did no reverence,   84
> Of my sovereyns gafe no fors at al,
> Wex obstinat by inobedience,
> Ran into gardyns, applys ther I stal ;
> To gadre frutys sparyd hegg nor wal :
> To plukke grapys on othir mennys vynes
> Was moor reedy than for to seyn matynes.

My luste was al to scorne folke and jape,   85
Shrewde tornys evir among to use,
To skoffe and mowe lyk a wantoun ape,
Whan I did evil othre I did accuse,
My wittys five in wast I did abuse,
Rediere chirstonys for to tell
Than gon to chirche or heere the sacry belle.

Loth to ryse, lother to bedde at eve,   86
With unwassh handys reedy to dyner,
My Pater noster, my crede, or my beleeve
Cast at the cok ; lo ! this was my maneere ;
Wavyd with eche wynd as dothe a reed spere,
Snybbyd of my frendys suche techechys for t' amende
Made deffe ere lyst nat to them attende.

A child resemblyng which was nat lyk to thryve,   87
Froward to God, rekless in his servise,
Lothe to correccioun, slouhe mysylfe to shrive,
Al good thewys reedy to despise ;
Cheef bellewedir of feyned truaundise ;
This is to meene, mysilf I cowde feyne
Syk lyk a truaunt felte no maneere peyne.

My poort, my pas, my foot alwey unstable ;   88
My look, myn eyen, unsure and vagabounde,
In al my werkys sodeynly chaungable :
To al good thewys contrary I was founde ;
Now ovir sad, now moornyng, ne jocounde,
Wilful, rekles, mad stertyng as an hare ;
To folwe my lust no man wolde I spare.

Our author states that he remained in this lamentable condition until he was "yeeris accountyd ful fifteene," and although he had become a religious :—

Duryng the tyme of this sesoun Ver,   80
I meene the sesoun of my yeerys greene,
Gynnyng fro childhood stretchithe up so fere
To the yeerys accountyd ful fifteene,
B' experience, as it was weel seene,
The gerisshe sesoun straunge of condiciouns,
Dispoosyd to many unbridlyd passiouns.

Entryng this tyme into religioun
Unto the plouhe I putte forth myn hoond,
A yeer compleet made my profession,
Considryng litil charg of thilke bond ;
Of perfectioun ful good exaumple I foond,
The techyng good in me was al the lak,
With Lootys wyff I lookyd ofte bak.

He was taught discipline by virtuous masters, and to follow
" blyssid Benyt " in doctrine. The rule was read and expounded
to him by " vertuous men religious and sad " ; but of all this,
though he " herd al weel ... of that they taughte," he took but
little heed. He wore a black habit of religion " oonly outward
as by apparence." To follow that change he " savouryd but ful
lite, sauf by maneer countirfet pretence." He feigned false
humbleness so covertly " when folkys were present, when as-
cending the ladder of the nine degrees of vertuous meeknesse,
called in the rule grees of humilitee," as to deceive everyone.
" While here in contemplaciouns I found but smal comfort,
Holy histories did to me no cheer,
I savouryd mor in good wyn that was cleer.
But a change for the better was at hand, for
Witheyne fifteene holdyng my passage,
Mid of a cloistre depict upon a wal
I sauhe a crucifix, whos woundys were nat smal,
With this word VIDE writen ther besyde,
" Beholde my meeknesse, O child, and lefe thy pride."
A circumstance to which our author attributes his reformation,
and of this word VIDE he, in his " last age taking the sentence,"
Gan to write with humble reverence,
In remembraunce of Cristis passioun,
This litil dite, this contemplacioun,
which is entitled " Lyk a lambe offryd in sacrifice." From this
period he seems to have seriously devoted himself to study
and to the service of the Church. We find that he was
shortly after sent from the monastery of St. Edmundsbury to

Gloucester Hall, Oxford (MS. Ashm. 59 ii.), it being the practice of the monastery to send all students for Oxford there ; while those intended for Cambridge were sent to Gonville and Caius College. Before the foundation of Gloucester College the Benedictines had no recognized college in the University for their novices, who were dispersed about in Houses. This Gloucester Hall was originally the property and residence of Gilbert Clare, Earl of Gloucester, from whom it passed to the Hospitallers of St. John of Jerusalem, and subsequently from them to the Benedictines. The College was supported by the contributions of the Abbeys of St. Edmundsbury, Glastonbury, and thirteen others, together with two priories, each of which, according to its position, sent two or three novices, who were maintained until they had graduated, and then returned to their monastery to teach their brethren. It was while staying at the University that Lydgate attracted attention as a poet, his translation of the fables of Æsop, entitled " Ysopus Ethiopus, in balade, by Dan John Liedegate, made in Oxenford " (MS. Ashm. 186) and many of his smaller pieces and ditties being written while there. On his return to the monastery of St. Edmundsbury he received his ordination. The Registry of Richard Braybrooke, Bishop of London, gives May 13, 1388, as the date of his receiving the four minor orders in the church of Hadham. The dates of his consecration to the Offices of Subdeacon (17 Dec. 1389), Deacon (12 May, 1392), and Priest (4 April, 1397), are given in the Registry of William Cratfeild, abbot of the monastery. (MS. Cott. Tiberius B ix. fols. 1, 35, 52. This MS. unfortunately nearly perished in the fire at Westminster in 1730, when so many of the Cottonian MSS. were either seriously damaged or entirely destroyed.) According to the custom of the time, Lydgate, in order to finish his education, left this country on a tour through France and Italy, but the precise date of his departure cannot be ascertained.

> I have been ofte in dyvers londys
> And in many dyvers regiouns,
> Have eskapyd fro my foois hondys,
> In cities, castellys, and in tons,
> Amonge folke of sundry naciouns,
> Wente aye forthe and took noon hede,
> I askyd no manere protectioun
> God was myn helpe ageyn al drede. (MS. Harl. 2255)

While abroad he made good use of his time, studying with diligence both the language and literature of France and Italy. On his return to England he opened in his monastery a school for teaching the youth of the nobility the arts of versification, &c. His mastery of the French language caused him to translate from that tongue into English verse a great number of well known pieces, which considerably enriched our literature, while causing the translator to make those amplifications to the English language for which he is regarded as a worthy successor of Chaucer. The Ashmolean Museum possesses his " Devowte Invocaton made by Lydegate to saunt Denys at the request of Charlles the Frenshe kynge to let it be translated out of Frenshe in to Englishe," and is also rich in the possession of other of his works. His oft quoted " Dance of Death " is derived from the same source.

> Out of the Frensh I dwight it of entent,
> Not word by word, but folwing in substance.

That he occupied a high position in the minds of the people at this period is proved by the titles prefixed to the various transcripts of his writings, as " that approbate poet," " that philosofre, Lidegate dann John," "that solempne religious Lidegate," " that vertuous Lydigate," " that solempne clerk," " the religious manne," &c. We find that he was still residing at the monastery in 1415, his name being mentioned in the register at this date in connection with the election of a new abbot —William of Excetre—Abbot Cratfeild having died in 1414.

But in June, 1423, he left the Abbey, being elected Prior of Hatfield Brodhook, Essex; in the following year, however, he had leave to return to his monastery again, preferring the quiet of his old cell to the more important position of prior. (Cott. Tib. B ix). Of the brilliancy of his genius and the depth of his learning there can be no doubt, for a slight glance at his voluminous writings will show that he was not only a good theologian and poet, in the true sense of the word, but a philosopher, geometrician, astronomer, and a logician.

In the Prologue of his "Story of Thebes"—which was intended as a continuation of "The Canterbury Tales" which had been left incomplete by the death of Chaucer—we have an interesting picture of him in his riper years. He says he travelled to visit the town of Canterbury

> In a cosse of blacke and not of green,
> On a palfrey slender, long slene,
> With rusty bridle made not for the sale,
> My man to foine with a void male.

He went "by fortune" to the inn where Chaucer's pilgrims had lodged, and the host addresses him thus :—

> Ye be welcome newly into Kent
> Though your bridle have nother boos ne bell,
> Beseeching you that ye will tell
> First of your name and what countre,
> Without more, shortly, that ye be,
> That look so pale, all devoid of blood,
> Upon your head a wonder threadbare hood,
> Well arrayed for a ride late.

He answered,

> My name was Lydgate,
> Monke of Burie, nie fifty yeare of age.

It appears that he more than attained the alloted three score and ten, for in the Harl MS. 2255 we have a metrical translation by him of the " De Profundis," to be hung against the walls of the Abbey Church, for the use of the monks, which he undertook at the command of Abbot Curteys, who died in 1446.

> Late charchyd in myne oolde days
> By William Curtys,
> Which gave comaundement
> That I shulde graunte myn assente.   (MS. Harl. 2255)

In his " Philomela " he mentions the death of an Earl of Warwick who also died in 1446. This brings our author to the age of seventy-eight, after which date little mention of him is anywhere made.

It is asserted on good authority that Lydgate was buried at St. Edmundsbury, and in MS. Harl. 116, fol. 170, occurs the following epitaph, written probably soon after his decease, but whether it is the same as that which graced his tomb is open to doubt.

EPITAPHIUM JOHANNIS LIDGATE, MONACHI DE BYRI.

> Lidgate Cristoticon Edmundum Maro Britannis,
> Boccasiousque viros psallit, et hic cino est.

Hæc tria praecipua opera fecit : vij libros de Christo, librum de vita Sancti Edmundi, et Boccasium de viris illustribus, cum multis aliis.

This epitaph, however, does not agree with that given by quaint old Fuller, which is as follows :—

> Mortuus seclo superis superstes,
> Hic jacet Lydgate tumulatus urnâ,
> Qui fuit quondam celebris Britannæ
>   Famæ Poesis.

And which has thus been rendered :

> Dead to the world, living above the sky,
> Intombed in this urn doth Lydgate lie,
> In former times famed for his poetry
>   All over England.

The assertion that "he was famed in former times" seems to imply that this epitaph was not written till a much later date than the year of his death.

In Vol. iv., p. 131, of the Archæologia appears an account of the discovery among the ruins of the Abbey of St. Edmundsbury of two fragments of coarse, soft stone with portions of an inscription upon them in which the name of Lydgate very clearly appears. An illustration of these interesting relics is given in the same volume. It is very probable that these pieces are portions of the original tomb of Lydgate, but the fragments of words that are upon them in no way coincide with any part of the epitaphs we have just quoted. This discovery, instead of putting an end to all doubts, only adds to our perplexity as to which must be regarded as the original inscription.

In the short sketch which we have given of the life of this illustrious monk we have purposely refrained from any criticism on his numerous works, our purpose being to notice these separately; but we will close this short biographical memoir by quoting the opinions of Fuller and the poet Gray upon his writings. The former says :—" If Chaucer's coin was of greater weight for deeper learning, Lydgate's were of a more refined standard for purer language, so that one might mistake him for a modern poet." Gray says : " I pretend not to set him on a level with Chaucer, but he certainly comes the nearest to him of any contemporary writer I am acquainted with. His choice of expression and the smoothness of his verse far surpass both Gower and Occleve. He wanted not art in raising the more tender emotions of the mind."

The Life of Our Lady.

THES booke was compilid by dan John Lidgate, monke of Burye, at the excitacion and steryng of oure worshipful prynce Kyng Harry the Fifthe, in thonoure, glorie, and reverence of the birthe of our most blessyd Lady, maide, wife, and moder of oure Lord Jhu Criste, chapitred and markyd after this table.

The Life of Our Lady.

Prologue.

 THOUGHTFUL herte, plonged in distresse,
With slombre of slouthe this longe wynt's nygt,
Out of the slepe of mortall hevynesse
Awake anone and looke upon the lygt
Of thilke sterre that with hire bemes brygt
And with the shynyng of hire stremes merye
Ys wonte to glade al oure emysperye ;
And to oppresse the derknesse and the doole   2
Of hevy hertes that sorowyn and sighen ofte :
I mene the sterre of the brygte poole
That with hire bemys whane she is alofte
May all the trouble aswagen and assofte
Of worldly wawys whych in this mortall see
Hath be bysette wyth grete adversite,
The rage of wiche is so tempestyous   3
That whane the calme is moste blandeschynge
Thane is the storme of deth most perilous,
Iff that he wante the lygte of hire shynynge,
And butt the sigte allas of hire lokynge,
From dethis brynke make us to ascape,
The havene of lyffe of us may nougt betake:

This sterre in beaute passeth Pliades,   4
Both of shynynge and of stremes clere,
Bootes Arcturus, and also Iades,
And Esperus whane it doth appere,
For this is Spica with hire brygte spere
That toward evene, at mydnyght, and at morowe
Downe from the hevene adaweth all our sorowe:
Whose brygte bemes shynen fro so ferre,   5
That clowdes blake may the ligt nougt steyne,
For this of Jacob is the faire sterre
That vnder wawes nevere doth declyne;
Whos cours is nougt undir the eclyptyke line,
But evere liche of beaute may be sene
A myddes the arke of our meredene;
And dryeth up the bitter teres wete,   6
Of Aurora after the morowe graye,
That she in wepynge doth on floures flete
In lusty Aprill and in fresshe May;
And causeth Phebus the brygte som's daye,
With his wayne golde-borned brygte and fayre,
To enchace the mystis of our clowdy ayre.
For this is the sterre that bare the brigte sonne   7
Which holdith ye septre of Juda in his honde,
Whos stremes ben out of Jesse ronne
To shede hire ligte both on see and londe;
Whos glad bemys withoute eclipsynge stonde
Estward to us in the Orient full shene,
With lygt of grace to voyde all oure tene.
Now faire sterre, O sterre of sterrys alle,   8
Whos ligt to see angeles delite,
So lete the golde dewe of thy grace falle
In to my breste lyk scalis faire and whyte,
Me to enspire of that I wolde endite,
With thilke bawme sente downe by miracle
Whane the holy gost the made hys habitacle.

And the sycour of thy grace shede 9
In to my penne to illumyne this dite,
Thourg thy supporte that y may p'cede
Sum what to seie in laude and pris of the ;
And first I thinke of thy nativitie,
So that thyne helpe fro me nougt twynne,
Benygne lady, anone for to begynne.

The Natibitie of Our Lady.

Cap. i   FLOURE of vertew, full longe kepte in clos 10
         Full mony a yeere with holsome leeves sote,
         Only by grace upon the stalke aros,
         Out of Jesse spryngynge from the rote ;
Of God ordeyned to be refuyte and bote
Unto mankynde, oure trouble to determine,
Full longe biforn by prescience divine :
The whiche flour p'serveth man fro deth 11
Unto the vertew whoso lyste take hede,
That in a gardyn a mydde of Nazareth
So faire som tyme gan to sprynge and sprede,
That thourg the worlde bothe in lengthe and brede
The fresshe oodour and also the swetnesse
Hertis comforteth of all hire hevynesse.
O Nazareth, wyth Bedleme the besyde, 12
This flour thou makyth of name more royalle
Than either Rome, elate and full of pryde,
Or mygty Troye, with the stordy walle,
Whos renoun holdith to be peregalle
In honor, prys, fame, or rev'ence,
Unto your passynge worthi excellence.

If for the fruyte comendyd be the tre,   13
Thowe hast more laude and comendacion
For thilke floure that sprong out of the
Than hath Aufrik, or worthy Scipyon,
Or Rome, or Cezar, or of Fabyon,
Thoug hire names were somtyme grave in golde,
Hir ydell fame to thyn may nougt be tolde.
Therfore reioyse and be rigt gladde and brygt   14
O Nazareth, of name most flourynge,
For out of the a floure most fayr of sygt,
Most full of grace, somtyme dide sprynge,
Of the whych fully remembrynge
So longe agon spake holy Ysaye
Whane that he seyde in his prophecye
That on this floure playnly shulde reste   15
The Holy Gost for his chosyn place,
As for the fayreste and also for the beste
That evere was, and most ful of grace,
Whos passyng beaute no stormes may deface,
But evere ylik contynueth fresshe of hewe
Withouten fadynge, the colour ys so trewe.
For this is the floure that God hym selfe behelde, 16
The whyte lylye of the chosyn vale,
The swete rose of the fayr felde,
Wiche of colour wexith never pale,
The violet, our langour to avale,
Purpul hewyd showith mercy and pite
To socoure all that in myschief be.
And frome the stocke of Joachym and Anne   17
This holy floure hadde hir original,
To him a forne by signe y-shewid whan
The Aungel tolde hem plainly that ther shall
Of hem be borne a mayde in speciall
Chosen of God, moost cheffe of her allye,
And for hire mekenesse hoote shal marye.

And whan the Aungel at the gate of golde   18
Hadde of this maide the birthe prophesyde,
And alle the manere of hem bothe tolde
In bookes olde as it is specifyed,
Hom to her hous anoon thei hem higed,
And she conseyveth, this faithful trewe wife,
By Joachim the holy fruyte of life ;
Oute of the wiche gan growe alle oure grace,   19
Oure olde sorowes oonly for to fyne,
The bytter galle pleynly to enchace
Of the venym callyd serpentyne,
For whan that Anna hadde monthes nyne
Boorne this fruyt so holy and entiere,
Thourg the grace of God anoon hit dyde appere
In the Oryent, to gladde alle mankynde   20
With dedly errour oppressyd of the nygt
With clowdes blake, and with skies blynde,
Tile they were cleryed with fayrenesse of the ligt
Of the wiche the Aungel somtyme hadde a sigt
With Jacob wrastlyng from him as he breide
So longe aforne to hym whan he seide
Lete me departe w^t outen more affray   21
Agens me and make noo resistence,
The nygt is passid, loo the morowe graye,
The fresshe Aurora, so faire in apparence,
Hir ligt daweth to voide all offence
Of wynter nygtis ful longe and tedious
With newe apperyng so glad and gracious.
This is to seye, the holy dawnynge   22
Of this mayde at hire nativyte
The nigt gan voide of oure oolde mornynge,
As the Aungel in fygure dide see
With such a touch made Jacob bee
Sore in his sinewes lych as it is founde
In thilke membre wher luste dothe moost hab'nde :

In figure oonly, that ther shulde sprynge   23
Doune by dissent oute of his kynrede
A clene mayde in wille and in worchynge,
Pure of entent bothe in thought and dede,
Whiche as Aurora, with hire rewis rede,
The nygt avoideth w⋅ hir copys donne
Afore the uprist of the brygt sonne,
Rigt so this maiden at hire nativitie   24
The nygt of dethe devoyded hathe awaye,
And brigte kalendys, moost lusty for to see,
Of Phebus uprist, with owte more delaye,
For she is Aurora, sothely this is to saye,
Oute of the wiche, as prophetys gan devyse,
The sune of life to us gan first aryse,
Of whose birthe ful many a day aforne   25
Albumazar rowte in speciall,
And seide a maide sothely shale be borne
Under the signe above celestiall
That callyd is the signe Virginall,
The wiche maide, as he eke telle canne,
Shal bere a chylde with oute spot of manne.
And as Mynerva, moder of prudence,   26
Is houlde a mayde, rigt so this hevenly quene
Bare in her wombe the Faders sapience,
And modre was and a mayde clene,
Of God p'videde pleynly for to beene
Socour to man and helpe in all oure neede,
Whan she was borne, this floure of womanhede.

How Oure Lady was Offeryd in to the Temple.

Cap.
ij ND aft' thre yeere, as was the usage,   27
Her moder pappys she lefte as in sowkyng,
And than anoon, in her tendir age,
Un to the Temple devoutly they her brynge,
And un to God they made offeryng
Of this maide, for to abyde there
With other maidens that in the Temple were.
And note with stondyng her passing tendirnesse,   28
Her grene yowthe, but of yeeres three,
Thourg Goddys helpe this braunche of holinesse
With outen helpe wente upe, gree by gree,
Fyfteen alofte, that alle mygten see,
To fore that auter of so grete an higte ;
And whane her moder therof hadde a sigt,
For verre ioye anoon she felle adoune,   29
And seid thus, that alle mygten heere :
God from above hathe herde my orison
Of his godenesse, and grauntyd me my preiere,
And recomfortyd myn opp'ssid chere
In sigte of hem that loughen at my peyne,
And of malice gan at me disdeyne.
Now hathe he be my singuler refuyte,   30
To my trestisse consolacioun,
For he hathe made the bareyn to bere fruyte
Thourg his mygty visitacioun,
And made clere my confusioun,
And alle my woo for to ov'goon
Oonly by grace amidde alle my foon ;

And thourg his migt the hertis hathe bowyd   31
Of hem that gan to chace at me by pryde,
Wherfor she hathe unto God avowyd
That hir dougt' shale in the Temple abyde,
The Hooly Gost for to beene hir guyde,
For ev'more by Goddis purviance
Thourg hir mekenesse him to do plesance.
Forthe alle hire lyff there to slepe and wake,   32
Him for to serve with humble parfitnesse
That alle maydens mygte ensample take
Of her allone to live in clennesse,
And specialy of hir devoute mekenesse,
Benigne poorte, countenance, and chere,
If that hem list of hire they mygte lere.
Fulle of vertue, devoyde of alle outrage,   33
Her herte was, that God to dwelle in chese ;
And day by day, rigt as she wexe in age,
Rigt so in vertue gan she to encrese,
And nygt ne day wolde she never cese
To exclude slouthe and vices to werrey,
With honde to worch, or w' mouthe to prey ;
For but in God her herte nougt deliteth,   34
So uppon him entirely was her thougt ;
And from above with grace he hire vesiteth
That ev'y thing but hym she sette atte nougt ;
Of worldly luste sche hathe so litell rougt
That oute of mynde she lete it ev' slyde,
That nougt but God may in her abyde.

Of the Conb'sacion of Oure Lady in the Temple.

Cap.
lij

ND whane that she v. yere dide atteyne   35
She was so sadde in conv'sacioun,
And as demure, sothely for to seyne,
From alle childhede and dissolucioun,
In gov'nance and in discrescioun,
And in talkyng as wise and as sage
As any mayde of thritty yeere of age ;
And of her rule this was her usance   36
From day to day, this hooly maide entere,
From pryme at morowe by continuance
Tille thre of the belle to be in her prayere ;
And tille the sonne was at mydday spere
On golde, and silver, and wolles softe,
With her hondys she wolde worche ofte ;
And ever at noone to brynge hir her fode   37
From God above ther was an aungel sente,
Wiche that she tooke as for her lifelode,
Thankyng him ay withe alle her hoole entente ;
And aft' meete anoon this maide is wente
Agen to preye til Phebus went to weste,
And ever at evene w⁴ hym she toke her reste.
This life she ledde, and this cours she gothe,   38
In whom was nev' yitt founde offence ;
And nev' man sawe this mayd oute wrothe,
But ev' meke, and fule of pacience,
Of hert clene, and pure of concience ;
This lyf she ledde, and as bookes teche
Of wordys fewe, and wondir softe of speche.

The meet also that was to hir brougt 39
Out of the Temple, for her sustinance,
With hert glad and a parfigt thougt
To poore and nedy, that lyvyd in penance,
To give it frely was alle her plesance ;
And who that ev' of her hadde a sigt
Of alle dissese was made gladde and ligt.

And ev'ry wigte greved w' sekenesse, 40
A touche of her made hem hoole anoone,
And thei that were in thougte and in distresse
Whan thei her seye hire malyce was a goone ;
And thus she was un to ev'ychone
Of alle meschief refuyte and remedye,
With a beholdyng of her goodly eye.

And of this maide, eke as it is tolde, 41
Here goodly face was so fulle of ligt
That noo man mygt susteyn to beholde,
For it was clerer than the sune brigt ;
That the crowne, in the wynt's nygt,
Of Adrian, ne of the sterrys sevene,
To her fairnesse ne bene nogt for to nevene.

Yitt nev' man temptyd was with synne 42
While he behelde on her goodly face,
The Holy Goost so holy was her withynne
That al enviroun sprede gan his grace
Where that she was p'sente in the place ;
For all weie God gaf to hire p'sence
So fulsome ligt of hevenly influence.

Ne noon so faire was nevere founde in Rewine 43
As was this maide of Juda and of Sione,
The dougter chosen of Jerusaleme,
Of David sede, to be sette aloone;
Of alle maidens, to reken hem ev'ychoone,
She bare the prise as well in fairnesse
As she excelled in v'tue and in goodnesse.

Lete be thou Grece, and speak not of Eleyne,   44
Ne thou Troie, of yonge Pollicene,
Ne Rome, of Lucresse with her eyen tweyne,
Ne thou Cartage, of the fresshe quene
Dido, that was some tyme so faire' to sene,
Let be your boste, and take of hem noon heede,
Whos beaute failleth as floure in frosty meede.

Hestir was meke but not to hir mekenesse,   45
And Judith wise, but she did yet excelle,
And Bersabe of grete semelynesse,
And Rachel fair, Jacob can you telle,
But she aloone of womanhede the welle
Of bounte beaute that nev'e fade may,
Nougt liche a floure that florissheth but in May.

Passeth echoone, bothe nyy and ferre,   46
Bothe in fairnesse and in p'fectioun,
Rigt as the sonne dothe a litel sterre ;
And as the rubye hathe the renoun
Of stonys alle, and dominacioun,
Rigt so this maide, to speke of holinesse,
Of women alle is lady and mastresse.

Of whom spake some tyme wise Salamon,   47
In Sapience who so liste to seeke,
That she was chosen for her self allon,
This white dove, w^t her eyen meke,
Whos chekes weren her beaute for to eke
With lilies meynte, and fresshe rooses red.
This is to sey, who so can take hede,

First with the roose of womanly sufferance,   48
And with the faire lilie next of chastite,
She was ennewid, to give her suffisance
As wel in goodnesse as in beaute ;
And as he seith, sche fairer was to see
Than other Phebus, Platly, or Lucyne,
With hornes ful of heven whene thei shyne.

And of this maide, as seint Anselme seith   49
In hys wrytyng, hir beaute to termyne,
Of face faire, but fairer yett of faithe
He seith she was, this holy pure virgine,
Whos chaste herte to nothing dide enclyne
For alle hir beaute but to holinesse ;
Of whom also this autor seith exp'sse,
That she was dougt' of David bi dissent   50
Sterre of the sea, and Goddys owne ancylle;
Quene of this worlde, al weie of oon entent,
And Goddys spouse, his hestis to fulfille,
And ev'e redy for to doo his wille ;
Cristis temple, and also receptakle
Of the Holy Goost and chosen tabernakle;
The Gate of Heven, and also the fairnesse   51
Of women alle who so loke a rigt,
Of maidenhede lady and princesse;
Oone of the fyve that bare her laumpys ligt
Redy to mete with her spouse at nigt,
Ful prudently awaiting at the gate
That for noo slouthe she come nogt to late.
In figure eke the chaundelabre of golde   52
That soome tyme bare vij laumpes shene,
This is to seye, the ressert and the holde
Of God p'servyd, for she was so clene,
Thourg her merite endowed for to bene
By grace of hym that is of power mooste
With the seven giftes of the Holy Gooste.

How Oure Lady resceived the vij Giftes of the Holy Goost.

Donum timoris Domini.

Cap.
iiij

HE firste gifte was the gifte of drede   53
To eschewe eche thing that shuld God displese.

Donum caritatis.

The next, pite of verre womanhede
To rewe on alle that she sawe in disese.

Donum scientiæ.

The thrid, konnynge God, and man to plese.

Donum fortitudinis.

The ferthe, strengthe thourg her stedfastnesse
Oonly by v'tue alle vices to oppresse.

Donum consilij.

Of conseille eke sche hadde excellence   54
To kepe hir pure in virginite,
For ay with conseille alied is prudence,
For God himself chese with hire to be.

Donum intellectus.

Of vnderstondynge eke the gifte hadde she.

Donum sapientiæ.

And of wisdom, so God list hire avance,
To know ev'y thing that was to his plesance.

Sche was the trone voyde of synne   55
That stant so ryalle in Goddys owne sigt,
To fore which sevene laumpis brenne
With hevenly fire, so spirituall of ligt,
That nevere waste but ylyk brigt
Conteñewen in oone liche above in hevene ;
By wych trone and the lampes sevene

Is undirstonde this maide moost entere,   56
With sevene vertewes that in hire were founde,
That some tyme weren with goostly ligt so clere
Thourg ligt of vertue inwardly iocounde,
Oonly thourg grace that dide in hir abounde ;
And alle thei weren groundid on mekenesse
Hire ligt to God more plesauntly to dresse ;
For faithe in hir hadde a grounde so stable   57
That it was voide of alle doubilnesse :
Hire hope of triste was also mayntenable,
Rootyd in God by parfit sekirnesse,
Whos charite so large gan him dresse
That up to God hastyd ranne the fire
With hert of clennesse to alle by desire.
Stronge in vertue, prudent in gov'nance,   58
She hadde also conveied with clennesse,
And soveraynly she hadde attempance
In alle her werkys w^t grace of visenesse
And evere anexèd vnto the rigtwitnesse.
With yn her herte of womanly bounte
She hadde of custome mercy and pite,
Sothefaste ensample also of chastite,   59
As seithe Ambrose, sche was in thougte and dede,
And trewe mirrour of virginite ;
Of poort benigne, fule of lowelyhede,
Ay humble of chere, and femynyn of drede,
Prudent of speche of what she list to shew,
Large of sentence and but of wordes fewe.
To preie and rede that was evere her lyfe,   60
Of herte waker by devocioun,
To God alle weie with thought contemplalif
Full fervent evere in hire entencioun,
And ydel nevere frome occupacioun,
And especially un to almes dede
Her honde was evere reedy at the nede ;

And fulc she was of compassioun 61
To rewe on alle that felte woo or smerte,
Wel willid ev' with hoole affectioun
To ev'y wigte, so lovyng was her herte.
Sadde w⁺ alle this that hire nevere asterte
A loke amys of here eyen faire,
So close of sigt was this debonaire.
And in psalmes ol holy p'phecie 62
To loke and reede she founde moste delite,
And whan she sawe and founde in Issaie
Of Cristis birthe howe he dide write,
To God she lifte hir tendir handis white
Besechyng hym that she mygt abide and see
The blesfule day of his nativite.
And in the booke of Elizabeth 63
That titillid is of her avisiouns,
I fynde howe this maide of Nazareth
Seide ev'y day sevene orisouns,
That callid ben her peticiouns ;
With humble herte this yonge blisfule maide,
Ful lowely knelyng, evene thus she saide :

𝕳𝖔𝖜 𝕺𝖚𝖗𝖊 𝕷𝖆𝖉𝖞 𝖕𝖗𝖆𝖎𝖊𝖉 𝖙𝖔 𝕲𝖔𝖉 𝖋𝖔𝖗 𝕾𝖊𝖇𝖊𝖓 𝕻𝖊𝖙𝖎𝖈𝖎𝖔𝖚𝖓𝖘.

Prima Peticio.

𝕮𝖆𝖕. BLISFUL lorde, that knowist the entent 64
𝖇　　　　Of ev'y herte in thyne et'nal sigt,
　　　　Geiv me grace the firste comaundement
　　　　To fulfille as it is skylle and rigt ;
And graunt also, with herte, wille, and mygt,
And alle my soulc, and alle my knowynge,
The for to love above alle othir thing.

Secunda Peticio.

A ND geiv me mygte pleinly to fulfille   65
 The nexte biddyng liche to thi plesance,
And for to love with herte and alle my wille
My neigebore in dede and countinance
Rigt as my self, with ev'y circumstance,
And here with alle, for ioye, woo, or smerte,
What thou lovest to love with alle myn herte.

Tertia Peticio.

T HE thridde precepte graunte eke, that y maie   66
 Fulfille also bothe erly and late
In suche manere as is moost to thi paie,
Benigne lorde, and make me for to hate
Mankyndes foo, for he made first debate
In kynde of man, and made him to trespace
Agenis the, and to lese his grace.

Quarta Peticio.

A ND, lord, graunte me for thi migte digne   67
 Above alle thinge to have mekenesse,
And make me humble, sufferant, and benigne,
With patience and inward myldenesse
Of alle vertues gev me eke largesse,
To be accepted the to queme and serve,
To fyn oonly thi grace y may disserve.

Quintia Peticio.

A ND also, lord, with quakyng hert and drede   68
 Mekely y preie unto thi deietee
Me for to graunt of thi goodlihede
The gracious oure for to abyde and see
In wiche the holy chosen maiden free
Into this worlde here aftir shal be born
Liche as p'phetis hav written here biforn ;

Howe that sche shal by thyn election   69
Be mayde and modir vnto thi sonne dere :
Nowe, good lorde, heere myn orison,
To kepe myn eyen and my sigt entere
That y may see her hooly halowid chere,
Her sacrid beaute and holy co'ntinance,
If thou of grace liste me so moche avance.

And kepe myn eren that I may also   70
Here hire speche and her daliaunce,
And with my tunge speke that mayden to
Paciently thourg her sufferaunce ;
Of worldly ioye this were my suffisaunce ;
And hire to love lyk as I desire.
Benigne lord, sette myn herte a fire.

And lord, also on me save thou vouche,   71
Thourg I ther to have no worthinesse,
That holy maide for to handel and touche,
(Myne owene lady and my mastresse)
And that y may w' humble buxumnesse
Vpon my fete, in al my beste wise
Goo vnto hir for to doo servyse.

And to that flour of virginite   72
Graunte also, lord, that y may have space
Mekely to bowe and knele vpon my kne,
Undir supporte oonly of her grace,
And to honour the goodly yonge face
Of her sone. as she dothe hym wrappe
In clothis softe liggyng in her lappe.

And love him best pleynly to my laste   73
With alle myne herte and myn hoole servysc,
With oute chaunge while my lif may laste,
Rigt as thi self, lord, canst best devyse,
So that I may in feithfull humble wise
In all this worlde no more grace atteigne
Than love him beste with all my mygte and peyne.

Sexta Peticio.

A ND to thi grace, lord, also I preie   74
 To graunte me to fulfille in dede
Hooly the statutys, and mekely to obeye
Within thi Temple, as y here hem rede,
For but thou helpe y may no thing spede
As of my selfe, and therfor vn to the
Alle y comytte as thou liste it be.
The observaunces and the p'ceptes alle   75
That to thi Temple, o lorde, ben p'tinent,
So lete thi grace by mercy on me falle
That y may doo hem w^t alle my hoole entent ;
And every biddyng and comaundement
That thi mynysters assigne vnto me
Make me fulfille with alle humilite.

Septima Peticio.

A ND thi Temple and thi holy house,   76
 Benigne lord, kepe me from damage,
And make thi peple to be v'tuouse
To thi plesance of ev'y maner age,
The for to serve with herte and hoole corage ;
And whan thei erre, lord, on any syde,
Er thou do rigt lete mercy ben hire gyde.

**How Abiathar, that year Bisshop of the lawe, wolde
have had Oure Lady weddid to his sone.**

Cap.   ND thus this maide al wey day be day   77
bi   In the Temple maketh her praiers,
     To plese God what she can or may,
     The chief resorte of alle her desires,
Tille she atteine to fourteen yerees,
With hert avowid bothe in thougte and dede
For to continue in her maydenhede.

Of whos entent God wote ful unware   78
Weren some of hem that in the Temple abide,
Of wiche a bisshop callid Abiathar
Caste him fully for to sette aside
Hire purpos pleinly, and for to provide
That hire avowe made of chastite
Shulde nougt holde, but vtterly that she
Shulde be weddyd sothely yif he migt   79
Un to his sone of heig affectioun,
For that she was in ev'ry wigtis sigt
So passyng good of condicioun ;
And to fulfille his entencioun
Abithar behoteth bothe goolde and rent
To the bisshoppis to make her assent
To this purpos, and to her thay gon,   80
And what they may thei gane her to excite
And to afferme to her everychon,
With suggered tunges of many wordis white,
That God above dothe him more delite
In birthe of children than in virginite,
Or eny such avowyd chastite ;
And more in children is honouryd in certeine,   81
And more in hem hathe he his plesance,
Than in suche as ben not but barreine
With oute fruyte thourg mysgov'nance,
And hooly writte maketh remembrance
That noo man was, sothely for to telle,
With oute seede blessid in Israelle.

How Oure Lady answered the Bisshoprps that she wolde not be weddyd.

Cap.
bij

O whom anon, wᵗ loke down cast and chere,   82
Benignely and in ful humble wise
This holy maide seide as ye shulle here :
Certis, quod she, yf ye wel you avise,
Wiche in yourself so prudent ben and wise,
And wel adv'rte in your discressyoune,
That Abel somtyme had a doubil croune,
Oon for his faithfulle trewe sacrifise   83
Offrynge to God of humble herte and free,
And another as y shale devyse,
For he his body kepte in chastite
And holy eke, as ye may rede and see,
For he in herte was a maiden clene,
He was ravysshid above the sterrys sevene,
Body and alle, in a chare of fire,   84
For he hym kepte frome al corrupcioun ;
Therfore in veyne is pleinly your desyre
To speke with me of this opynyon,
For God wel knoweth myn entencion,
How I have vowyd as it to hym is couthe
To be a mayde fro my tendyr youthe,
And alle my life so forthe to p'sev'e   85
For life or deth oonly for his sake,
From wiche purpos y shale not dissev'e,
Thourg his grace, whether y slepe or wake,
To kepe and houlde y have undertake
Mi maidenhede sithen yoo ful yore,
Agen wiche ne speketh to me noo more.

And whan thei seyen her hert not mutable,   86
But ever stedfast of oon affection,
And ev'yliche as any centre stable,
Thay have made a convocacion
Of alle the kynredis in conclusion
The eigte day to come in fere
By oon assente to trete of this matier.
This is to seye that of oolde usage,   87
Of custome kept for a memorialle
That ev'y maide xiiij yeere of age,
Riche and poore, of the stocke rialle,
In the Temple no lenger dwelle shalle,
But by statute shale be take and maryed
By the lawe and noo lenger taryed.
And whan thei were assemblid alle in oon   88
Isacar in open audience
Ganne to p'nounce afore hem ev'ychone
Fulle prudently the some of his sentence,
And seid, Siris, with your patience
So it youre eeris offende not ne greve,
Declare y shale my menyng w^t your leve.
Yif ye remembre sithe Salamon the kyng   89
In Israell cepter bare and crowne,
In this Temple so rialle in bildyng
Have yonge maidens bi devocion
Of custome hadde here conv'sacion,
Bothe kynges dougters and p'phetys eke,
As ye may fynde yif ye liste to seke,
Vn to the age of fourten yeere   90
Abiden here, and noo lenger of space
As ye wel knowe, w^t oute any were,
And than ben removed from her place
And in her stede other dide pace,
As custome was, and eche in her lynage
Deliv'ed was vn to mariage.

And as a lawe it hathe be kept ful trewe　　91
Vnto this tyme in hie and lowe astate,
But nowe Marie hathe founde an order newe
To kepe her clene and inviolate,
Agens wiche ther helpeth noo debate
For of free choise and hertly volunte .
She hathe to God avowed chastite.

Wherfor me seemeth it were rigt wel sittyng　　92
To this purpose by good discrescion
Firste that we mygte fully have knowyng
Of Goddis wille in this opinion,
For then it were more p'feccion
Her clene entent as semeth me
And eke the strenger of autoryte.

———◆◇◆———

Þow Ioseph was weddyd to Oure Lady.

Cap.
biłj

IRST that we mygte knowe v'rely　　93
To whos kepyng she shale co'myttyd be :
And thai assenten here to v'rely
Withouten more of hige and lowe degree ;
And of accorde and of oon unite
The prestys alle bigonnen to p'cede
To caste lotte downe by eche kynrede,
The wiche lotte felle on Juda anoon,　　94
As I suppose thurg Goddis purviance.
And Ysacar amonge hem ev'ychone
Pourposed hathe a newe ordinance,
That ev'ry wigte of that alliaunce
That wiflees were w^t oute more delay
Shulde brynge a yeerd agen the nexte day.

And to the bisshop, higest of echoone 95
Everiche of hem dide his yeerde brynge,
Amonge wiche Joseph hadde brougt oone
Thoug he were oolde and paste his likyng,
And he anoon made his offeryng
To God above and a sacrifice
In the oolde lawe suche as was the guyse.
And God to him did anoon appere, 96
And w' the yerdis bade that he shulde goon
And put ev'rychone in feere,
In sancta sanctoru' liggyng oon bi oon,
And on the morowe to come agen echon
Ev'iche his yerde to resseme agen,
And upon wiche openly were seyne
A dove appere, and up to heven flee, 97
He shal have, w' oute moore obstacle,
Marie in kepyng, so faire upon to see,
As it is rigte, for the hige miracle :
And whan thay come to the tabernacle
As ye have herde, the bisshop devoutly
Ev'iche his yerde deliv'ed by and by,
But utterly upon noon of them alle 98
At thilke tyme was ther noo thing seyne,
For Goddys heeste was nougt yit yfalle
Of her desire to putte hem in certeyne :
Wherfor the bisshop with newe fire ageync
Entrid is in to the seyntuarye.
And while that he a while gan there taryc,
Goddys aungel apperith to him newe 99
Doune fro heven by miracle sent,
And tolde playnly the heeste of God was trewc,
And howe himself was some what necligent
For to delivre by comandement
Ev'y man his yerde as he ougt.
And whan the bisshop arigt him bethougt

He gan remembre plainly in his mynde   100
That of disdeine and wilfulle necligence
The yerde of Joseph was lefte behynde,
Wherby he knewe that he hadde done offence,
And gan anoon to brynge it in p'sence,
And toke it Joseph devoutly in his honde
Amonge hem alle ther thei dyde stande.

Alle behinde, dissev'ed from the prees,   101
With humble cheere in the lowist place, .
And of his yeerde in manere recheles,
Fulle stille of porte, with a dredful face ;
And whan he dide with his honde embrace
His yerde agein, fule debonaire of looke,
For innocence of humble drede he quoke.

And sodenly thourg grace above divine,   102
Alle ppenly in ev'y wigtis sigte,
Vpon the yerde of Joseph ful benigne
Was seene a dove, of fetheris lilie white,
That toward heven evene toke the fligt, .
And with oon voyse the peple thoo abreide
And vn to Joseph alle at onys seyde :

Blessid art thou and blessid ys thi chaunce,   103
Thy face blessid, and thine aventure ;
And blessid is thi humble attendaunce,
And thou art blessid so longe to endure
For to possede so faire a creature,
So good, so holy, now in thi passing age,
So gracious, so benigne, so wise and sage.

And she anoon by preestys of the lawe   104
Assigned was vn to his gov'nance,
But sely Joseph gan him thoo wᵗ drawe
With humble chere and shamfast continance,
And seid, Certis, ther is noon accordance
Bitween her youthe, flouryng in fairnesse
And me whom age with unlust dothe oppresse,

For she is faire and fresshe as rose in May,⸱ 105
And wel y wote also a maiden clene ;
And y am oolde, wᵗ white lockes graye,
Passid ful ferre my tendir yeeres grene ;
Wherfor y praie you to consider and seene
To accorde discordant seith to me no more
Bitween her beaute and my lockes hoore.
And whan the bisshop sawe the humble entent 106
Of this Joseph and the innocence,
And how that he to take her nolde assente,
To him he seid in open audience :
Joseph, he seide, take heed to my sentence,
And be wel ware that thou the not excuse
Ageyn the wille of God for to refuse
This hooly maide assigned vn to the 107
By opyne signe whiche alle the peple seye,
Thourg Goddis grace and mygti volunte,
Agen wiche be ware to disobeye,
And thenke howe he some tyme made to deye
Abiron and Dathan oonly for the offence
Doon vnto him of inobedience.
Quod Joseph, that wile y not in noo thing 108
To Goddys wille ne biddyng be contrarye,
But her accepte in to my kepyng,
For whom God hathe shewid signes faire,
Whiche is so good, benygne, and debonaire,
That y to her wole servant be and guyde
Til God for her list bet to provyde.
And as the custome of the lawe hem bonde 109
So made was the confirmacion
By heest of wedlok bytwen hem honde in honde,
And he her toke to his possessioun
With hert clene and meke affectioun ;
But while he wente to Bedleme the citee
Mary abode stille in Galilee,

How Joseph aft' he hadde weddid Oure Lady wente to Bedleme and usid the crafte of carpentrye.

Cap. ix

AT Nazareth, in her faders house, 110
Liche her avowe of hert alweye in oone.
And fyve maidens the moost vertuous
Of the Temple were chosen oute anoon
Of the bisshope w^t here for to goone
To wayte on her by humble attendaunce
In what thei canne to serve and do plesaunce,

Of wiche the firste callyd was Rebecca, 111
And Scephea the secunde as y fynde,
Susanna, Gabel, and Abigea
The tother thre, as bookes make mynde,
Wiche wolde nev' thourg slouthe be behynde,
But ay in oone, as hit is specified,
In werke and praier were occupyed.

And vn to hem, as is made mencion, 112
That of lyvynge so feithfulle were and trewe
And diligent in occupacioun,
Deliv'ed was silke of sondry hewe
For to make div's werkys newe
In the Temple of intencioun
Oonly to be in mynystracion.

And as it is putte in remembraunce, 113
Evr'che her silke toke by aventure
Liche as her honde fel ther on by chaunce ;
But Mary, as thoo God shope her evre,
The purpil silke toke in her care
Of gracious happe of soorte with oute sigte,
The whiche colour of custome and of rigte

To noon estate is kyndely fittyng, 114
Of duete to speke in special,
But to the state oonly of a kyng,
So that no wigt but of the stocke rialle
By statute oolde this colour vse shalle,
For by oolde tyme ye sholde noo man seen
In purpil clad but outher kyng or quene.
Wherfor the sorte ful rigtfully ys falle 115
Verrely by dewe disposicioun
Vpon Marye that before hem alle
By lyne rigt is dissendid don
Of blode riale, and bi election
Of God above was chosen for to been
For her merite of heven and erthe queen,
And moder eke, as ye shal after here, 116
Of thilke kyng that clad was alle in reede
Of purpul hewe, both face and chere,
Doune to the foote fro his blessid heede,
Whane he of purpil dide his baner sprede
On Calvarye abroode vpon the roode
To save man kynde whan he ther shedde his bloode.
And of this purpul that y speke of to forne, 117
I fynde pleynly how that Mary wrougte
Thilke vayle that was on tweyne torne
The same houre whan he so dere vs bougte,
Loo how that God in his eternal thougte
Provydid hathe by iust purveaunce
The purpul silke to his moderis chaunce.

How Oure Lady ys sette for an ensample of birginite.

Cap.
I

UT now y leve this blessid maide dere   118
In Nazareth amonge her frendys to dwelle,
Ledyng a life more parfite and entiere
Than any tounge suffice may to telle,
For evyn like as a fulsome welle
Shedith hir stremys in to the rivere
Rigt so Marye an ensamplere cleere
Gave vnto alle by plenteuous largesse   119
Oonly vertu vppon ev'ry syde ;
O wel were thei to whom thou were mastresse
And blessid eke that mygt on the abide
To have by exaumple so virtuous a gide ;
And blessid was that holy companye
That daye by daye the seien with her eye ;
And blessid was the paleis and the house   120
In wiche thou haddyst thi holy mansion
Fortuned wel and wonder gracious,
So humble was thi conv'sacion ;
And blessid was also al the ton
There thou abode, and blest be the village,
O hooly maide, where thou haddist hostage ;
And blessid was the worthi table riche   121
Where day be day thou wentist vn to boorde,
For in sothenesse the ioye was not liche
Of Cersus kynge, for alle his riche hoorde ;
And blessid be thay that herden worde by worde
Of thi speche ; and blessid the houre and tyme
Of alle thi life from evene til the prime.

O weelful eke and gracious the sigt   122
Of hem that mygten vpon the beholde,
For wel thei oute to·be glad and ligt
That were with the alweye whan thei wolde ;
And blessid weren yonge and oolde
That weren reioiced with thi excellence
Whan that hem liste of the hige p'sence.
Of the joie whoo coude telle arigt   123
Of thine hevenly meditaciouns,
Assendyng vp above the sterrys brigt
In thine ynward contemplaciouns ;
Or the hooly visitaciouns
Who can reherse, brigt as sunne or levene,
So ofte sente don to the fro hevene.
Or who can telle thi hooly slepys softe,   124
With God alweie fule in thi memorye,
For love of whom thou sigedist ful ofte
Whan thou were soole in thine oratorye ;
Or who can telle the melodie and glorie
That aungels hav made in the place
For the ioye thei hadde to looke in thi face.
I am to rude to rehersen alle   125
For vnkunnynge and for lake of space,
The mater is so inly spiritual
That y dare not so hige a stile pace;
But ladye myne y putte all in thi grace,
This first boke compilid for thi sake
Of my symplenesse, and thus an ende y make,
Besechyng alle to have pite and routhe   126
That therof shullen have any inspection
Yf ougte be lefte of necligence or slouthe
Or seide to myche of p'sumpcion,
And putte it mekely to her correction,
And aske mercy of my trespase
Ther as y erre, and putte me in her grace.

And thourg her benigne supportacion   127
So as y canne forthe y wole p'cede
With alle myn herte and hoole entencion,
Prayng that maide of so goodly hede
Croppe and roote to helpe in this nede,
Whom y nowe leve in Nazareth soiourne,
And to my mater y wole agein retourne.

END OF THE FIRST BOOK.

How Mercy and Pees, Rightwitnesse and Trouth dispu-
tiden for the redempcion of man kynde.

Cap.   HO that is bounde and feteryd in prison   128
xi   Thenketh longe after deliverance ?
            And he that felith payne and passion
            Desireth sore after allegiaunce ?
And who that is in sorowe and penaunce
Little wondre of hertly hevynesse,
Thourg he coveyte relese of his distresse ?
And who that lyveth in langour or in woo   129
Fer in exile and prescripcioun,
And is with sette w^t many a cruel foo,
And can noo gyvve to his salvacioun
To ascape dethe w^t oute greete raunson,
Ful longe he thenketh of ful litil space
While he in bondys abideth after grace

And yitte to recorde of oolde felicite   130
In soothfastnesse encresith moore his payne
Than alle the constreynt of his adv'site,
And causeth him more to sige and playne,
For ioye passid can hertys more constrayne
Here welthe aforne to bywepe and waile
Than alle torment that dothe hem assaile.
O who coude ever sith the worlde bygan   131
Of more ioye or of gladnesse telle
That some tyme coude the worthy kynde of man
That shapen was in Paradise to dwelle
Till he, alas ! was banisshed in to helle,
Fer in exile from his possession,
And ther to abyde stocked in prison.
And he hathe lost his richnesse and honour,   132
His myrthe, his ioye, and his oolde welfare,
His force, his mygte, and hooly his socour,
And was of vertu nakyd made and bare,
And lay fule sike languisshing in care,
So far p'scripte oute of his cuntre
That by the lawe ther may no recov'e be :
Whos necke opp'ssid with so stronge a chene   133
Lay plunged downe w^t oute remedye,
That whan M'cy wolde have bene amene
Rigtwitnesse anoon gan it denie :
And whan that Pees for recov'e gan to crye,
Came Trouthe forthe with a sterne face
And seide platly that he gete noo grace ;
For Pees and Mercy to gider assemblid were   134
Fulle longe agoon to trete of this matiere,
And Rigtwitnesse with them was eke there,
And Trouth also with a denyous chere :
And whan thai weren all foure in feere,
As ye hav herde, and ganne to entrete,
Than furste of alle cruelly to threte

Trouthe began, al mooste in a rage　　　135
Of cruel ire and of malencolye,
And seide shortly that man for his outrage
Of verre rigt moste nedys dye.
And thus began the controu'sye
Betwene the Sustren, and Trouthe alwey in oone
Seide plainly that recure was ther noone,
For I, quod Trouthe, at his creacioun　　　136
Telde him the perelle affore his offence,
But he me putte oute of his bandon
And gave to me no man'e audience.
And I, quod Rigt, with alle my diligence,
Wolde him have rulyd, but he ne toke noon hede,
Wherfore of me he gete noon helpe at need :
And whan he gave credence to the snake,　　　137
He made his querelle even agens Rigt,
And agen Trouthe he falsly gan to take
Whan he her putte clene oute of his sigt :
And agen Pees began a quarelle to figt
Whan he from hym Mercy sette aferre,
Brekyng the trewer and wolde algate have warre.
Therfor, quod Rigt, pletyth for him no more,　　　138
But lette him have as he hathe deservyd,
Ye doo grete wronge yif ye wile him restore
That hathe his heest to you not conservyd.
A yis, quod Mercy, Nature hath reservyd
To Pees my sustre plainly and to me
On wretche ever to have pitee,
And he offendid hathe of ignorance　　　139
More than of malyce, y wys, quod M'cy, thoo.
Ye for alle that he moste have his penance,
Quod Rigt anoon, liche as he hathe doo.
A thenke, quod Pees, that toward Jerico
He was dispolid amonge his cruelle foone
For lacke of helpe whan he lefte him alloone.

That was, quod Trouthe, for he was recheles 140
To goo the waye I taugte him of resoun.
Quod Mercy, than the mortal too of Pees,
The oolde serpente, roote of all tresoun,
Of false envie and indignacioun,
Lay in a wayte to brynge him in a trayne
Whan he to him falsly dide fayne
That yif he eate of the forboden tree 141
The faire fruyte in Paradise p'sente,
He shulde like vn to goddys bee,
Of good and yvele to have the entendement :
And for my sustir Trouthe was absent,
And ye yourself also Rigtwitnesse,
He was betrayhed slyly bi falsnesse.
Wherfor, quod Mercy, y purpose vtterly 142
Him to releve yif y can or may ;
And y, quod Pees, wole helpe faithfully
The greete ire and rancour to allay
Of Judgment to putte it in delay ;
And here vpon, to finde ful refuge,
I wolde p'cede afore the hige Juge.

———

Þoto Mercy and Þees brougte this Þlee before the Þige Juge.

 Cap. xij AND rigt forth with befor the kynge of glorye 143
Mercy and Pees the cause brougte anoon,
And in the hige hevenly consistorye
Pees seide thus amonge hem ev'ychone :
O blessid Lorde, that art bothe thre and oone,
So plese it The benignely to here
What y wole seye, and my sustir dere.

Remember, Lord, amonge thy werkys alle   144
How thou madist Mercy sovereigne,
That whan that ever vn to the she calle
Thou maist nougt of rigt her praier disdeyne,
And specially whan that we bothe tweyne
To thine higenesse for any thing requyre,
Thou muste of grace fulfille oure praier.
Is nougt thi mercy greet above the hevene,   145
Thine oune dougter cheef of thin allie,
And hathe her place above the sterres sevene
With the orders of every ierachye,
Whom, day by day, thou canst so magnifie
Amonge thi werkys to make her empresse
To helpe wretchys whan thei been in distresse?
Thi mercy eke abideth ever w^t the   146
Liche thi gretnesse and thi magnificence,
And who that dothe mercy and pitee
Dothe sacrifice hige in thy p'sence;
And is not mercy of more excellence,
Liche as the Sawter wel reherse can,
Vpon the erthe thanne the life of man?
Thi selfe also, as it is playnly couthe,   147
Avisely who so taketh hede therto,
Seist opynly with thyne owne mouthe
That to a thousand thou canst thi mercy doo;
And holy David recordith eke also
With his harpe above alle thinge
That he thi mercyes eternally shale synge.
And hou mygte eke any creature   148
Vpon erthe, in any maner kynde,
Without mercy any while endure?
For alle were goon yif mercy were behynde.
Wherfor, Lord, on mercy have thi mynde
The woofule caityf to take vn to thi grace
That so longe hathe be sev'yd from thi face.

And thoug that y be humble, meke, and free 149
Forsothe, Lord, of duete and of rigt,
Yit evere in oone my dwellyng is with the
For seelde or nevere y parte oute of thi sigt,
Pees is my name, that power hathe and mygt
Thourg my konnyng hem that ben mortall foone
By the helpe of the to accorde in to oone.

And also, Lorde, as holy writte can telle, 150
That of thi pees ther may non ende be,
And eke thi pees dothe ev'ry wigte excelle
And art thi selfe of verre duete
Callyd the prince of pees and vnyte,
And yit behoteth wretches to releve,
That is mankynde, and shal nev' from them meve :

And Joob recordeth the holsomest fruyte 151
Of alle this worlde spryngeth oute of pees.
Now, Lord, sithe y am made to be refuite
And to the wofule comforte and encrees,
Graunte of thi grace nowe a fulle relees
That y and Mercy may the foone confounde
Of thilke caitif that lieth in prison bounde

So that he may have liberte 152
To goo at large, and have remission
Of this thraldome and captivitie,
And be deliv'yd oute of his prisoun
So that ther may be made redempcion
For his servage and a finall pay
Lord of thi mersy w^t out more delay.

And whan thei hadde hire mater ful purposyd 153
Mercy and Pees with ful hige sentence,
Touchyng man with synne so envoisid,
The juge gave benigne audience ;
And whan he hadde longe kepte silence
For alle the skilles to him that thei laide,
Yet at the laste to hem thus he seide :

How God the fader of heben answerd to Mercy and Pees.

Cap.
xiij

YNE owne dougtir next to myne allie,   154
Thoug youre requeste come of tendir herte
Ye mote consider with a prudent ye
Of Rigtwitnesse it may not me asterte,
Liche youre axinge by favour to adv'te
Vnto the cause that ye rep'sente,
But Rigt and Trouthe fully wolde assente,
Withouten whom y may not p'cede   155
To execute any maner iugement,
Wherfore lete calle hem in this greete nede,
For y moste werche by hire avisement.
And whan thei were come and p'sent
Thanne Trouthe anoon touching this matier
Seiden opynly that alle mygten here :
Yf it so be this man that hathe trespast   156
Ne be not dede for his iniquite
Than vtterly the fraunchise is depast
Bothe of my sister Rigtwitnesse and me,
And fynally oure bothe liberty
Gothe vnto nougt and oure jurediction
But he be punnysshed for his transgression.
The worde of God, that pleinly may not erre,   157
Telde him aforne withoute any drede
The grete perelle of this mortall werre,
Etcynge the appill that he mote be dede,
But he of slouthe toke ther to noon hede,
Wherfor he must. as rigt list p'yde,
With owt m'cy the doome of dethe abide.

And thoug that Pees be of pite mevyd 158
Man to deliv'e with a zeele of routhe,
Rigtwitnesse wolde than be agreved
With me to consente that am callid trouthe,
And as me semyth it were to greete a slouthe
Doome or cause plee or any sute
With outen us tweyn to ben execute,
Me seemeth eke my suster Pees dothe wronge 159
To foster a Man and holde agen us tweyne,
That hathe ben co'versaunt so longe,
Amonge us discorde to restreyne.
Therfor, quod Pees, now wole y not feyne
To do myn office rigt to modefye
That she of rigour cause him not to dye.
Than, quod Rigt, of necessite 160
Hit muste folowe thoug he were my brother
That he mote dye by doome of equite
Or in his name mote be dede some other :
So of my schippe guyd ys the rothir
That I ne may erre for wawe or for wynde
More than the anker of trouthe wole me bynde.
Certys, quod M'cy, so it not displese 161
Un to youre wise and noble prudence,
His dethe to you may be littl eese
For holy writte reherseth in sentence,
Yif ye consider in youre advertence,
That deeth of synners the hige God to queme
Is werste of dethis yif ye of rigt list deme,
For synful blode ys noo sacrifice 162
To God above that every thing may seyne :
Than muste ye the dethe of oon devyse
That is of synne innocent and clene,
And as y troue undir the sune shene
Thourg oute the worlde, to reherse al mankynde,
Hit were fulle hard suche oone to fynde,

For ruste with ruste may not scouryd bee   163
Ne foule with filthe may be purified,
And who is soilid with dishoneste
To wasshe a nother as it is not aplied
Blak in to white may not be undied,
Ne bloode infecte with corrupcion
To God for synne ys noon oblacion.
Figure herof yee may behoulde and see,   164
As the Bible maketh mencion,
How that a lamb of spotte and filthe free
Some tyme was take by eleccion
And offerid up in satissfaccion
To God for synne, for to signifie
That who that shulde for manys raunson dye
Muste be clene, pure, and innocent   165
Rigt as a lambe from ev'y spotte and blame :
And trewly undir the firmament
Ther was noone suche sithe Adam dide ataine
The fruite to eete for either halt or lame
In sov'eigne vertue is al the kynde of man.
Wherfor, quod Mercy, the beste rede that y can
That Pees my sustir sese this discorde   166
And alle the strife that is bitwene,
And that we prei our juge and mygty lord
To this matier benignely to seene
And of his grace to shape suche a mene
For Truth and Rigt so prudently ordeyne
That Pees ne y have cause to pleyne.
And this request is nougt agens Rigt   167
Ne un to Trouthe pleynly noon offence
Yif that oure juge of his grete mygt
Ordeyne so in his providence
To shape a weie thourg his sapience
That Trouthe and Rigt be not displesid
Thourg Pees and me thoug man be holpe and esid.

Howe the Fader of hebene oonyd thise iiij Sustrenne.

Cap.
xib

ND whan that she had by reson fined   168
That groundyd was pleinly vpon skylle
The hige Juge by Mercy is enclined
To condescende of grace to her wille,
And in oudre wise her axynge to fulfille,
That Rigt be servyd and Trouthe not dismaied,
That Pees and she shullen eke be wele apaied.
And by sentence anoon diffinitif   169
The Juge seide for conclusion :
An innocent pure and clene of life
Shale mekely dye to paie the raunson
For mannes gilte and transgression,
And he so frely shale the dethe obeie
In al his peyn that he noo word shal seie.
And thus shale Rigt in alle man'e thinge   170
Have her desire and Trouthe shalle not faile
To execute fully her axynge   .
Finally to stynte this bataille.
And for that Pees so moche may availe
And Mercy eke shale not be agrevyd
Her bothe axinge shale also be achevyd.
To finde a man that shale undirtake   171
This migti querel of mercy and pitee
To suffer dethe oonly for manys sake,
Uncompellyd freely of volunte,
That as a lambe with oute spotte shal be,
And with his blode shalle wasshe vndefoulyd
The gilte of man with ruste of synne y-moulyd

Howe the Fader of hebene tolde these liij sustryn how hys oone childe sholde take mankynde.

Cap.
xb

UT for to wote of what stock he shal sprynge,   172
Of what kynrede and of what astate,
My sothfast worde eternally lyvynge,
Myne owne sonne with me increate,
Shalle don be sente to be Incarnate,
And wrappe him selfe in the mortal kynde
Of man for love so that he may finde
A clene grounde his paleice on to bilde   173
In alle the erthe, nother of lyme ne stoone,
But in a maide debonaire and mylde,
The humble dougtir of Juda and Sion,
And vnto her shalle Trouthe and M'cy goone
By oone accorde sente afore my face
Liche my devyse to chese me a place,
And seie to her in alle man'e thinge   174
Her tabernacle that she make faire
Agen the comynge of her mygty kynge,
Whiche is my sonne and myne owne aire,
That in her breste shale have his repaire,
Where Trouthe and Mercy shulle to gyder mete
By oone assente and her rancour lete,
And ther shal Pees kisse Rigtwitnesse,   175
And alle the sustirs accorde in oon place,
And Rigt shalle leve alle her sturdynesse,
And Trouthis swerde shalle no more manace,
And finally Mercy shalle purchace
A charter of pardoun liche as this maide clene,
And whiche for man be so goode a mene

That he shalle nowe ascape daungerlees   176
Amid the forest free from ev'y trappe,
While the maide that causeth alle this pees
Hathe the vnicorne slepyng in her lappe,
That thourg mekenesse shal his horne so wrappe
Ther it was wont to slee by violence.
Thourg dethe it shal agen dethe be diffence,
Agenis venym more holsome than triacle,   177
Every poyson asofte and asswage,
Whan the lyon maketh his habitacle
Wyth in a maide but of tendir age,
And Gaubriel shalle goon on message
To her anoon, myne owne secretarye,
With new tydynges, and noo lenger tarye.

Howe Gaubriel was sente to Oure Lady.

**Cap.
xbi**

AND rigt forth wᵗ the aungel taryeth not,   178
But hilde his weie from the see of glory
Vn to this maide clene in wille and thougt,
Where as she sate in her oratorye
With hert ententif and wᵗ hoole memorye
Erecte to God and alle her fule mynde,
To whom the aungelle whan he dide her fynde
Benignely with alle humilite   179
Seide vnto her anoon as ye shullen here :
Heile, ful of grace, our Lorde is with the,
Ne drede the nougt but be rigt glad of chere
That art to God so acceptable and deere,
That hoole his grace is vpon the falle
To be moste blessid amonge women alle.

And with that worde, thourg grace of Goddys mygt, 180
Al hoole the sunne of the deite,
That from heven his blissful bemys brigt
Shadde on the erthe of oure humanite,
Whan in the breste of a maiden free
The Holy Goost by free election
For her mekenesse hathe made his mansion.
For whan that Bernard some tyme gan beholde 181
With thougt uplifte by contemplacion,
The brigte sune in hert he gan to colde,
Inly astonyed in his aspection,
And ful devoutely in a meditacion,
Thereof remembryng as he gan take hede,
Seide even thus quakyng in a drede :

———•••———

A Lamentacion of Seint Bernard.

 Cap.
xbij

LORDE, quod he, y am a gryside, 182
And sore a dredde to loke on this clernesse,
And yit wel more with feere y am supprisid
For to beholde for myne unwirthinesse
Any worde to write or to expresse
Of this misterye and great privitee,
Benigne Lorde, lest thou seie to me
What, art thou bolde or darst in any wise 183
My Rigtwitnesse to telle or to wrigte,
Or to presume so hardely to devyse
Mi testament with thi mouthe endyte :
That certys Lord, but yif thou respyte
My wretchednesse by supporte of thi grace
I greetly drede of dethe for my trespace.

But wolde God thourg his greet mygt 184
And his goodnesse liche to my desire
That from auter that brenneth in his sigt
Noo litil sparkle but a flamme of fire
Wolde don dissende my herte to enspire
For to consume with his fervent heet
The rusty filthe that in my mouthe dothe ficte.
And all unclenness cankered ther of oolde 185
To make clene and to scoure aweie,
That thourg his grace y durst be so bolde
Other to write other some worde to saye
That was rehersyd vppon the blissfulle daye
Whan Gaubriel and Mary mette
In Nazareth, and humbly her grette.
But sithen this man so parfite of lyvynge, 186
This holy Bernard, so good and gracious,
So dredfulle was this matier in writyng
That was of life so inly vertuouse,
How dare y thanne be p'sumptuous,
I, woful wretche, in any maner wise
To take on me this parfite hie emprise,
My lippis polute, my mouth w^t synne ysoilid, 187
My herte vnclene and fulle of cursidnesse,
My thougte also with alle vicys foylid,
My breste rescette and chest of wretchidnesse,
That me to write of any parfitnesse
Not oonly drede of p'sumpcion,
But for to encurre the indignacion
Of God above for my greet offence, 188
That y am bolde or hardy in his sigte
To dare presume the grete excellence
For to discribe of her that was so brigt ;
But undir hope that mercy passeth rigt,
And that disdeine my stile not nor werrey,
With humble herte thus to him y prey :

𝔄 Recapitulacion of the 𝔚ordys of 𝔊aubriel to 𝔒ure 𝔏ady.

𝔈ap.
xbiij

LORDE, whos mercy gothe not to decline, 189
But ev'y liche stondyth hoole in oone,
That some tyme sentyst don fro' Seraphyn
To Isaie an aungel with a stoone
Wherw⁴ he began to touche his mouthe anoon
To purge his lippis frome alle pollucion,
So lete thi grace to me dissende a don
My rude tounge to explite and speke   190
Some what to seie in comendacion
Of her that is welle of womanhede,
And thourg her helpe and mediacion
Be to my stile fulle direction ;
And lette thi grace alweye be p'sente
This booke to further after myne entent,
For of my selfe to vndirtake   191
To speke or write in so devoute matere,
Litel wonder thourg y tremble or quake
And chaunge bothe continance and chere,
Sithen this maide of vertue tresorere
Pturbyd was in looke and in visage
Of Gaubriel to here the message,
And ful demurly stille gan abide,   192
And in her herte castyng up and don
Fulle prudently vpon ev'y syde
The maner of this salutacion,
And howe it mygte in conclusion
In any wise fully p'formyd be,
She stondyng hoole in her virginite.

And whan the aungel sawe her lowlyhede,   193
And the hooly reednesse also in her face,
He seide, Marie, for noo thinge that thou drede,
For to fore God thou hast fcunden grace,
And shalt conseyve within a litel space
And in thy wombe a sone of alle vertu,
And shalte him calle whane he is borne Ihu,
That shale be grete and namyd sothefastly   194
Sone of the higest that ever was of mygt,
And God to him shalle give seete ful iustly
The se of David, his oone fadirs rigt,
And he shal reigne in ev'y wigtis sigt
In the house of Jacob eternally by lyne
Whos kyngdom ev'e shale laste and nev'e fyne.
And thoug his heeste were passyng of rennon,   195
Surmountyng eke as in excellence,
That vtwardly gaf so m'veilous a son
And wondirfulle to her audience,
Yit she ful mekely of grete rev'ence,
And looke doncaste of her yen clere,
Benygnely the aungel gan enquere
In what maner shale this thing betyde   196
Sithen y noo man knowe in noo degree.
Quod Gaubriel, within thi blessid syde
The Holy Goost shale y thronyd bee
And alle the vertue of the Trinite,
Enclose shalle in thi breste so clene
The sune of life with alle his bemes shcne.
Wherfor this childe that shal of the be burne   197
Shalle callyd be Goddys sone entere.
Beholde and see a litel here to forne
Elisabeth, thin owne cosyn deere,
Conseyved hathe sithen goon half yeere,
Thoug she for age wente to have be bareyn,
And is w^t childe to putte alle in certeyn

That to God is no thing impossible   198
But as him liste may ev'y thing fulfille
Vnto whos worde be fully nowe credible.
Biholde, quod she, of God the meek ancille
With alle my herte obeying to his wille
In ev'ry thing rigt as him liste it be
And liche thi worde falle it vn to me.
Loo she that was chosen for to been   199
Of alle the worlde lady and emp'esse,
Of heven and erthe allone to be quene,
And Goddys moder for her holynesse,
Loo for alle this howe lowely w^t mekenesse
She alle comitteth vn to Goddys wille
And as he ordeyneth redy to fulfille,
And nolde calle her selfe noon other name   200
But Goddys handmaide in fulle lowe man'e.
O where is all the transitorie fame
Of pompe and pride and surquedrie in fere,
Where is youre boste or daren ye appere
With youre forblowyng vanyte,
Sithen that a maide thurg her humilite
Of pride hathe nowe wonne the victorie   201
And openly hathe given him a falle
Thourg whoos lownesse the hige kyng of glorie
Within her wombe hathe made in specialle
His dwellyng place and his hospitalle,
And with oon worde of the maide y-spoke
The Hooly Goost ys in her breste y-loke.

Howe hooly men of divine licnessys wrote of Oure Lady in comendacion of her.

Cap.
xix

ND whan the aungel fro her dep'tyd was,   202
    And she allone in her tabernacle,
    Rigt as the sune percith thourg the glas,
    Thourg the cristal birell of spectacle,
Withouten harme, rigt so bi miracle
In to her closet the faders sapiencé
Entrid ys withouten violence
Or any weme vn to her maidenhede   203
On any side in party or in alle,
For Goddys sone takyng our manhede
In her hathe bilte his paleis principal,
And vndir pigte this mansion rial
With seven pillers as made in memorie,
And therin sette his reclinatorie,
Wich is p'formyd al of pure golde,   204
Oonly to us for to signifie
That he alle hooly made hathe his holde
Within this maide that callyd is Marie;
And seven pillers that shulden this maide gie
Been sevene spiritis, so as y can disserne,
O God above, this maide to governe,
For alle the tresour of his sapience,   205
And alle the wisdome of hevene and erthe ther to,
And alle the richnesse of spiritual science,
In her were shitte and closid eke also,
For she is the toure, withoute wordys mo,
And house of ivor in wiche Salamon
Shitte alle his tresour in his possession.

She was the castelle of the cristalle walle   206
That nev' man mygt yit unclose,
In wiche the kyng that made and causeth alle
His dwellyng chefe by grace gan dispose.
And liche as dewe dissendith on the roose
With silver droppis, and of the leves faire
The fresshe beaute ne may nogt appeire,
Ne as the rayne in April or in May   207
Causeth the vertue to renne oute of the roote,
The greete fairnesse ne appeire may
On violettys and on herbis soote,
Rigt so this grace of alle oure grevous boote,
The grace of God amydde the lely white,
The beaute causeth to be of more delite.
And as the cockle w^t hevenly dewe so clene   208
Of kynde engendreth white peerlys rownde,
And hathe noo cherisshyng but the sune shene
To his fostryng, as it is plainly founde,
Rigt so this maide of grace moste abounde
A peerle hathe closid with in her brestys white
That from the dethe mygt alle oure rannson quyte.
She was eke the gate w^t the loke brigt   209
Sette in the northe of hige devocion,
Of wiche some tyme the p'phete had a sigt,
Ezechiel in his avisioun,
Whiche stode ev' close in his conclusion,
That nev'e man entre shale ne passe,
But God him self to make his dwellyng place.
And yit in sothe, as y reherse canne,   210
So as the flyse of Gedeon was wette,
Tofore he fawte with hem of Madian,
With hevenly dewe enviroun alle by sette,
In signe oonly he spede shalle the bette,
Rigt so hathe God on her his grace shewid
With the Hooly Goost whan she was al be dewyd,

In token playnly she shulde socoure be   211
Vnto mankynde manly for to fygt
Agen the devyle that hathe in his pouste
Alle Madian with his felle mygte,
And thourg the helpe of this maiden brigt,
And thurg the dewe of her hevenly grace,
We shulle this serpente from our bondes chace.
She was also of golde the riche urne   212
Kepyng the man of oure salvacion,
That alle oure woo may to joie turne
With holsome foode of p'fection;
And eke she was in signification
The yeerde of Aaron w^t fruite and leves lade,
Of vertu most to comforte vs and glade.
She was the auter of cedre, golde, and stone,   213
Stedfast and trewe of p'fection,
And as the cedre conservyng ay in oone
His body clene from alle corrupcion,
And for to make a fulle oblacion
Of ev'y vertue to God in chastite,
She shone as golde by parfite charite.
And on this auter she made her sacrifice   214
With fire of love brennyng as brigt
To God and man in ev'y man'e wise
As doon the sterrys in the frosty nygt;
Her frankensense gaft so clere a ligt
Thourg good ensaumple that the parfit levene
Of her lyvyng raugte unto hevene.
She was the trone where that Salamon   215
For worthinesse sette his rialle see,
With golde and ivor that so brigt shone
That al aboute the beaute men may see,
The golde was love, the ivor chastite,
And twelfe lyonns so grete huge and large,
That of this werk bare up the charge,

Of the oolde lawe weren p'phetes twelfe   216
That longe biforne gan behoulde and see
That Salamon, Goddys sone him selfe,
Shulde in this maide beholde his riall see,
So that in sothe her clene virginite
To be a modir shulde noo thing lette,
Amydde her brest he his troone sette.

She was also the woman that seint John   217
Sawe in hevene so richely appere,
Cladde in a sune, the wiche brigter shoone
That Phebus dothe in his large speere ;
And twelfe sterres that passingly were clere,
So as to him plainly dide seme,
Weren sette above in her diademe.

And as him thougte at her feete ther stode   218
A large mone brigt and no thing pale,
In figure oonly that she that is so good
To swage the bitter of our oolde bale,
The svnne of life made to avale
Dovne to the erthe to gov'ne vs and guyde.
And eke the moone to us dothe signifie

Alle hooly chirche large to biholde,   219
Whiche in this maide hadde hir originall,
Whan finally with his rightis oolde
The sinagoge of Jewys hadde a falle,
For in this maide the firste faithfule walle
Of hooly chirche God gan first to bilde
Whan w't his sone he made her goo w't childe.

And to reforme the rudenesse vtterly   220
Of blynde folkys that konne not parceyve
Howe that Marie mygt kyndely
A maide be and a childe conseyve,
That yif him liste resoun to conseyve
That may examplis rigt y nowe fynde
Of this mater accordynge vn to kynde.

Auti̇k conclusions agenis bnbileful men that seien that Crist mygte not be borne of a maide.

Cap.
II

BLYNDE man that thurg thin iniquite   221
Why haste thou loste thi reson and thi sigt,
That thou of malyce list not for to see
How Crist Ihu thurg his greet mygt
To his disciples helde the weye rigt
Thourg the gatis shitte by greet deffence
Without brekyng or any violence?
Whi mygt he nougt of his magnificence   222
Within a maide make his mansion,
And she yit fonde in hige excellence
Of maidenhede from all corrupcion?
Ye ben to blynde in youre descrescion
That liste not see also how he roose
From dethe to life and his sepulture close.
And here w^t alle thou maist also adv'te   223
Howe he fulle graciously of his mygty grace
Made Peter oute of prison sterte,
And where him liste freely for to pace,
And yit the dorys were shitte of the place.
What wondir than thoug that God by miracle
Within a maide made his habitacle,
And beyng cloos and parfitly shitte   224
With alle the boundys of clene virginite,
So sothefastly her clenness was not lette
Vpon noo side ne her chastite
But incresid and fairer for to see
That Goddys sone liste to ligte a don
Within this maide to make his mansion.

Eke Hildefone telleth of a tree   225
In stede of fruite that berith briddys smale
From yere to yere by kynde as men may see
Withoute medlyng of female or of male,
This verrely is sothe playnly and noo tale;
Than wonder not thoug Criste were borne bitwen
The chaste sydys of a maiden clene.
Eke certeyn bryddys called vultures   226
Withoute medlyng conseiven by nature,
As bookes seyn w^t oute any leese,
And of her life an c yeere endure ;
Than the lorde of every creature
That causeth alle noo wondir thoug y seide
Thoug that he were conseyved of a maide.
And Plunius in bookis natural   227
Write of a roche grete and large also
That will remeve w^t a fynger smale,
But yit a man doo alle his mygt therto
Hit wole not steere nether to ne froo,
Rigt so this maide that is of vertue moost
With a fynger of the Hooly Goost,
And with a touche of his mygti grace,   228
Conseyved hathe stedfast God and man,
That nev' mygt remeve from her face
Of thilke avowe that she first began
To be a maide as ferforthe as she can
In hert and wille as any roche stable
That from his grounde is not remeveable.
This clerk also, this wise Plunius,   229
Seithe in Tauriche ther is an erthe founde
That of nature is so vertuous
That wole cure ev'y man'e wounde,
Rigt so Marie was the erthe sounde
That God oute chese bi eleccion
To bere the fruyte of oure redempcioun,

That shulde be helthe and also medecyne 230
To alle oure woundes whan thei ake or smerte,
And oure greves and oure hurtys fyne,
From dethe to make vs to asterte
With holsome bawme p'ceyng to the herte,
That shale to helthe sodeynly restore
Our festryd soorys that thei shulde ake no more.

And fourther more, this auctour can eke telle, 231
Within his booke who so loke a rigt,
To Jubiter sacred is a welle
That whan it hathe queynte the brondis brigt
That este agen it gevith hem a newe ligt,
Who liste assaie sothe he shalle hit fynde.
What wondir than thoug the God of kynde

Amyddis the welle from filthe of synne coolde 232
Fulle of vertue wᵗ faire stremys clere
His loggyng toke and his mygty houlde,
And thourg his grace sette it newe afeere
With the Holy Goost that wᵗ outen were
She brente in love hatter than the glede
Thoug she were coolde from alle flesshlyhede.

And in Ffalisco, as him liste to writte, 233
Is a welle that causeth eke of newe
Whan ther drinken oxen to be white
And sodeinly for to change her hewe,
What mervayle than thoug the welle trewe,
The welle of helthe and of life eterne,
The lorde of alle, so as y can disserne,

His stremes shedde into this maide free 234
To make her whigtest as in holynesse,
That bothe shulde maide and modir be,
And ev' in oone kepe her clenness
Withouten change, so that her whigtnesse
Ne fadeth never in beaute ne coloure,
Of maidenhede to bere bothe leef and floure.

And who that wolde dispute in this matier　　　235
I houlde him madde or els oute of mynde,
For yif he have his ygon hoole and cleere
He shale nowe see preefs y vowe be kynde,
For he that made bothe leef and cynde,
And with a worde this waste worldys wilde,
Migte make a maide for to goo wᵗ childe.

And he that made the hige cristal hevene,　　　236
The firmament, and also ev'y speere,
The golden axtre and the sterres sevene,
Citherea so lusty for to appere,
And rede Marce wᵗ his sterne chere,
Migte he not eke oonly for oure sake
Within a maide of man the kynde take ?

And he that causith foulis in the aire　　　237
In her kynde to waxe and multiplie,
And fisshe eke with fynnes silver faire
In deep wawes to gov'ne hem and guyde,
And dothe on lyve and an othir deie,
And giveth beestis her foode vpon the grounde,
And in her kynde dothe hem to abounde,

Sithen he is lorde and causeth alle thinge　　　238
To have beyng, yif y shale not fane,
And is the prince and the worthy kynge
That alle embrasith in his mygty cheyne,
Why mygt he nogt by power sov'eigne
At his free chois, that alle may save and lese,
To his modir a clene maide chese ?

Who causeth the fruite of the harde tree,　　　239
By vertu oonly that spryngeth from the roote,
To growe and wexe, liche as men may see,
With levys grene and newe blossomes soote,
Is it not that lorde that for our alther bote
Wolde of a maide, as y reherse can,
Mekely be borne wᵗ oute touche of man ?

For he that dothe the tendir braunchis sprynge   240
And fresshe flourys in the grene mede,
That weren in wynter deede and eke droupinge,
Of baume voide and of lustihede,
Migte he not make his greyn to growe and sede
Within her breste that was bothe maide and wife,
Wherof is made the sothefast brede of life ?
And he that graveth of his greete mygt   241
Withoute poyntel in the harde stone
And in the tabullys w^t letters clere and brigt
His ten p'ceptys and biddyngis ev'ychone,
The same lord of his power allone
Hathe made this maide here in erthe lowe
A childe conseyve and no man to knowe.
And he that made the bushys to appere   242
Alle on flawme w^t feery sparcles shene,
And whan Moisis gan to approche nere,
And yit noon harme come to the bowis grene,
The same lorde hathe conservyd clene
His habitacle and his herber swete
In this maide from alle flesshly hete.
And he that made the yerde of Moises   243
Of a serpente to take the liknesse
In the halle amonge alle the prese,
Where Pharao the pepul dide opp'sse ;
And in the disert, the bibul berith witnesse,
The ryver made renne oute of the stone
The thriste to staunche of the pepul anoon :
And over this for to verefie   244
His grete mygt, Sampson the stronge man,
As Judicum dothe plainly specifie,
Dranke the water that from the chawle ranne :
And he that made the floodys of Jordan
To turne agein for love of Josue,
That alle his pepul cleerly mygt sce,

And howe wawys a sondre gan breke   245
And liche an hille to stande hige alofte :
And he that made the asse for to speke
To Balaam for he roode so softe,
Whi mygt he not by power p'vyd ofte,
Sithe he the yren made in the watir hove,
Be of a maide borne for mannys love ?
And he that made an aungel for to take   246
Abucuk by a litille heere
And sodenly brynge him to the lake
In Babilome which was so ferre :
And to vesitte, lyggyng in his feere,
Danyel amonge the bestys rage,
Til he to him brougte the potage,
The dourys shitte of the stronge prison,   247
For to aswage of hunger alle his payne,
And in a moment to his mansion
Fulle sodenly restoryd him agene :
Why mygt he not as wel in certyn
The same lord of a maide than
Take flesshe and bloode and bicome man?
And he that made the svnne at Gabaon   248
To stonde and shyne vpon the brigte shilde
Of Josue, and toward Achalon
The moone also, as the hoost bihelde
The longe day thei faugte in the feelde
Agenn the kynges of mygty Ammorre,
That his peple clerly mỹgt see ;
And he that made the shade to retourne   249
In the Orlage of kyng Ezechie
By ten degrees oonly to parforme
By heest ymade to him of Issaie,
Whi migt he not, this lorde that alle shal guye,
Of a maide by the same skille
Freely he borne atte his owne wille ?

And he that fedde w^t v lovys smale   250
Five thousand in solitarie place,
Ffer in deserte sittyng in a vale,
Thurg the foison and plente of his grace,
The same lorde, why mygt he not purchace
Within a maide duryng her maidenhede,
Whan that him liste to take his manhede ?
For as the bee bothe wexe and hony shede   251
At the hyve, who taketh hede ther to,
Rigt so Marie, flouryng in maidenhede,
Bare in her wombe God and man also
And yit in sothe she was bothe twoo
I dare afferme in oon p'sone in feere
A maide clene and Cristis modir dere.
And as the Beeme shynyng from so fer   252
Shedith his ligt as men may wel espie
Withouten harme or hyndryng of the sterre,
And so as Manna fel don fro the skye,
Rigt so this floure that callyd is Marie
With wombe halowid in to chastite
Conseivid hathe in her virginite.
And as the Bernake in the hard tree   253
Of kynde bredith and the vyne flour,
Causeth the wyne florre for to be,
Thurg Bachus mygte as grapes gov'nour,
Rigt so in sothe mankyndis savyour,
As the barnak and floure oute of the vyne,
Spronge of Marie she beyng virgine ;
And as a worme vndir the hard stoone   254
Of the erthe cometh w^t oute engendrure ;
And as the ffenix, of wiche ther is but oon,
To ashes brent renueth by nature,
Rigt so this lorde that alle hathe in his cure
Oure kynde agein from synne to rennewe
Toke flesshe and blode in this maide trewe.

And as the snowe from Jubiter dothe falle   255
Thurg the force of Sagitarius bowe,
And Zepherus dothe the flowris shale
On white blossomys whan she dothe blowe,
Rigt so in sothe the grace aligte alowe
Of the Holy Goost, like a wynde cherisshyng,
Amidde the maide to make his dwellyng,
And to the floure did noo duresse   256
But parfitly conservyd hir beaute
From ev'y storme of flesshly lustinesse,
I liche fresshe of fairnesse for to see
As by examples moo than two or thre,
As ye toforne have herde devyse,
Whiche as me semyth ougte ynow suffise
To alle that ben groundyd in the feithe   257
Agens falshede to stonde at diffence.
And yit in sothe, as seint Gregorie seith,
Feithe hathe noo meryte where as evydence
Or manys reson geveth experience,
But he that leveth and fyndeth noo reson
Ne kynde accordyng is worthi more guerdon,
But if that any be nowe in this place   258
That hathe doute or ambiguite
Thurg false errour that dothe his hert embrace,
Either of malice or of iniquite,
For to accuse the virginite
Of Marie, pleinly this is my boone.
But yif so be that he amende soone
And axe m'cy for his grete offence   259
Of her that is of m'cy grownde and welle,
That he of vengeance have exp'ience
With Ixion don depe in helle,
And that the clappere of his distuned belle
May cancre sone, I mene his fals tunge
Be doumbe for ever and nev'e este be runge,

With hym I am no bet in charite 260
Than ye have herde, at even and at morowe,
For here my trouthe he get no more of me
Save Cerberus y take him to borowe
What ever he bee and leve him w^t sorowe
To Tantalus his hunger to appese,
At fewe wordis passe over is an ese.

How Oure Lady went to John Baptists modir.

Cap.
xxi

OR what in sothe vpon any syde 261
Is Phebus chare aperrid of his ligt,
Thoug ygen rawe may not abide
For to behold agenis his bemys brigt,
Rigt so pleynly thourg the gowndy sigt
Of eritekes may not susteine
For to beholde the clennesse of this quene,

May in noo wise sothely disencrece 262
Her clere ligt ne her parfit brigtnesse
Whos faire stremys shullen never sese
Without eclips to shine in clennesse,
For of this maide as bookes seyn exp'sse
Whan Gaubriel to hevene drowe the coost
She replenisshid of the Holy Goost

Roos up anoon, and oute of Nazareth 263
Toward the mounteyns faste gan her hyee,
And ther she salweth mekely Elizabeth,
Within the house of trewe Zacharie ;
And rigt forth with whan she dide espie
Of Marie the meke salutacion,
And thourg her eris whan passed was the son,

Within her wombe, pleynly this no tale,   264
For verrey ioye and spiritual gladnesse
The yonge Infaunte with his lymes smale
Reioisid him, the Gospelle dothe exp'sse ;
And sche fulfillid in verre sothfastnesse
With the Hooly Goost lowde gan to crye
And evene thus seide vnto Marie :
Blessid art thou amonge women alle,   265
And of thi wombe blessid the fruite also,
And howe to me of happe is nowe bifalle
Mi lordis modir for to come me to,
For verrey ioie y not what y may doo,
For sothefastly thi gretyng as y heere
Within my wombe my litil child nowe here
Reioiseth him for gladnes as he can,   266
That of alle woo myne herte it dothe releve.
And blissid art thou that first this ioie began
The worde of God so faithfully to byleve,
Nowe be rigt glad and thin herte meve
For alle thinges shale p'formyd bee
That been of God behestid vn to thee.
Marie than with a devoute entent,   267
With looke benyngne and ful humble chere,
The same houre being ay p'sente
Elizabeth, her owne cosyn deere,
With alle her herte anoon as ye shale heere,
And alle the accorde and hoole melodie
Of the Holy Goost, seide in hir armonye :

How Oure Lady made Magnificat.

**Cap.
rriɟ**

WITH laude and price my soule magnifieth   268
Eternal lorde, both oon, two, and three,
That alle athe made and ev'y thing nowe gieth,
Wiche of his mygt and bountevous pite,
Of his goodnesse and hige benignite,
Oonly of m'cy liste to have plesaunce
For to consider and graciously to see
To my mekenesse and humble attendaunce;
Mi spirit also with hert and thougt in feere   269
Reioisyd hathe with fulsome habundance
In God that is my sov'eigne herte entere,
And alle my ioye and alle my suffisaunce,
Mi hole desire and alle my sustinaunce,
Within my thougt so depe he is grave
That but in him with oute variaunce
In alle this worlɟe y can noo gladnesse have,
For he from heven goodly hathe biholde   270
Of his handmaide the humilitee,
Wherof in sothe al oonly for he wolde
Alle kynredys shalle blessid calle me,
Of wiche the thanke, O lorde, be vnto the
With preise and honour of ev'y voice and tunge,
Thurg armonie of sothfast vnite,
For this allone be to thi name sounge,
For he to me hathe doo thinges grete   271
Of hige renoun and passyng excellence;
His grace made so fully to me flete,
For he is mygty of his magnificence,
His name hooly and most of rev'ence,
That while I leve it shalle me nev'e sterte
With alle my trewe faithful diligence
To thanke him of alle myn hoole herte.

And he his m'cy moost passyngly famous   272
From kyn to kyn, and so don to kynrede,
Shale thurg his grace be so plentevous   ·
Perpetuelly that it shale p'cede,
And specially to hem that louen and drede
Mine owne lorde with herte wille and mynde,
To suche his pitee shale ever sprynge and sprede
Of dewe rigt and nev' be byhynde ;
He hathe his arme enforcid and made stronge   273
His dredfule mygte that men may see and knowe,
And proude men thei reigne not ful longe,
He seuerid hathe and made hem falle lowe,
With alle his herte don of the whele hem throwe
For to abate hir sirquidrie and pride,
Or thay were ware her pompe was al ov'throwe
Ful sodeynly and leide her boste aside,
And mygty tyrauntis from her rialle see   274
He athe avallid and y-putte a downe,
And humble and meke for her humilitee
He hathe enhaunsid to fulle hige renon,
For he can make a transmutacion
From lowe to hige, as it is seyn ful ofte,
And whan him liste the dominacion
Of worldly pompe to falle ful vnsofte ;
He hathe fulfillid and fostrid in her nede   275
With the goodis of plenteuous largesse
Hem that weren hungry and indigent in drede,
And hem relevyd of alle her wretchidnesse ;
And he the riche hathe raugt from his richesse
Fulle wilde and waste to walke vpon the pleine,
And sodenly him ploungid in distresse
Al solitarie and lefte him ligge in veyne,
For he his childe chosen of Israel   276
Benignely hathe taken to his grace,
And of his mercy is remembrid welle
To voide oonly vengeance from his face,

And humble pees shale occupie his place,
And pite shal be feffid in his stalle,
And trouthe shale his rigt so embrace
To sette mercy above his werkys alle,
As he hathe spoken and faithfully bihigte   277
To oure fadirs that hav ben her to foore,
To Abraham and to his sede of rigte,
That his mercy shal laste ev'more,
For nere his mercy alle the worlde were lore,
Vn to the wiche to make man atteyne
He hathe made m'cy oure kynde to restore,
And of alle his werkys to be sov'eigne.

How Oure Lady aft' the byrthe of seinte John Baptyst torned to Nazareth.

Cap.
xxiij

ND whan this blessid ditee   278
Was seide to God devoutely of Marie,
I fynde after playnly howe that she
Stille in the house aboode of Zacharie
Thre monthes, the Gospel may not lye,
And after that y reede in certeyn
To Nazareth that she wente agein
And ther aboode in contemplacioun,   279
In her praiers alle wey day by daye,
With many an hooly meditacioun,
To queme her lord in what she can or may,
From whom her thougt went nev' away,
Her ful mynde, ne her remembrance,
For but in him she hathe noo plesance

In alle this worlde of noo man' thinge   280
For alle her ioye was on him to thenk,
What ev'e she dide preiyng or worchynge,
Noo thing but he mygte in her herte synke,
For finally whethir she wake or wynke
Amydde her hert he was al weie p'sente
So fixe on him was sette her hoole entent.
And day by day this holy life she ladde,   281
This parfite maide thurg hige devocion,
So feruent love vn to God she hadde,
Ther may be made noo division
For she sequestrid her opinion
From alle the worlde and lette it pleynly goon
So hoole to God she gafe her herte allone
For ever in love she brente more and more   282
Toward God in his hige servyse
Was alle her luste w^t herte sette so soore
Alle erthely thing she fully dothe dispise,
And day by day her wombe gan to rise
Thurg the fulfilling of the Hooly Goost
Therin by loke whom she loved moste.

GLOSSARY.

Abreide, A.S., to awake, to start
Abroode, A.S., abroad
Adaweth, A.S., awakeneth
Aforne, A.S., before
Aire, heir
Albumazar, an Arabian astronomer of the 9th century (?)
Algate, A.S., always, although
Alther bote, greatest good
Anoon ⎱ by and bye
Anoone ⎰
Ancille ⎱ LAT., maidservant
Ancylle ⎰
Aspection, sight
Assofte, to soften
Astoneyd, A.S., confounded, astonished
Asswage ⎱ A.S., to assuage, to
Asswagen ⎰ sweep away
Asterte, A.S., to escape, to release, to alarm
At, that
Attempance, temperance
Auter, altar
Autor ⎱ A.N., author
Auctour ⎰

Autentyk, powerful
Autik, authentic, reliable
Autoryte, A.N., authority; a text of Scripture or some recognised writer
Avance, A.N., to advance, to profit, advancement
Avallid, A.N., to cover, to let down
Avise, advice, counsel
Ay, A.S., ever
Bale, A.S., mischief, sorrow
Bandon, A.N., dominion, power, subjection
Behoteth, to become, to be the duty of
Beforn ⎱
Biforn ⎰ A.S., before
Biforne ⎰
Ben, A.S., inf. m. to be; pr. t. pl. are; p.p. been
Bernake, the barnacle goose
Bersabe, Bathsheba
Bette, adv. com. for better
Bihigte, called, promised
Bigonnen, A.S., p.p. begun

Bootes Arcturus, the brightest star of the constellation Ursa Major

Bote, medicine, remedy

Brede, a board, broad, width

Breide, attack

Bounte, bounteous

Brenne, burn

Bryddis, birds

Cercus, Crœsus, king of Lydia

Chawle, a jaw

Chese, A.S., to choose

Citherea, the star Venus

Conclusyon, determination, judgment

Conveied, recovered

Coost } NORTH. loss or risk, to
Cost } tempt

Copys } A.N., a cloak, a vest-
Cope } ment

Couthe, pa. t. of conne, knew, was able ; p.p. known

Cynde, A.S., natural, kind

Daliaunce, toying, wantonness

Dan (LAT. Dominus), lord, a title common to monks

Debonaire, A.N., gentle, courteous

Digne, A.N., worthy, disdainful, proud, dignity

Dissense, strife, quarrelling

Div's, divers, several, sundry

Doole, A.S., sorrow

Donne, A.S., of a dun colour

Dougt', daughter

Duresse, hardness or hardship, severity, confinement

Eclyptyke, the ecliptic, or great circle of the heavens

Eche, A.S., each, every

Echon } each one
Echoone }

Eke, A.S., also

Eleyne, Helen

Enlumine, A.N., to illuminate, to enlighten

Envoisid, comforted, encouraged

Enviroun, A.N., around, to beset

Entent, A.N., intention

Ennew } to paint, to put on
Ennewed } the last colours

Entendement, understanding

Ensample } example
Ensaumple }

Emysperye, the hemisphere

Er, A.S., before, before that

Eritekes, heretics

Esperus, the evening star

Eterne, LAT., everlasting

Ev' } every
Ev'y }

Even, of Efen, A.S., evening

Ev'iche, A.S., each one, every one

Ev'yliche } ever the same,
Evereliche } always alike
Evereylik }

Ev'ychone, every one

Explite, accomplish, perform

Fabyon, Fabius

Ferthe, fourth

Feere, A.S., a companion ; in fere, together, in company ; fear, to terrify

Feffid, obtruded, placed

Flete, drop

Florre, flower

Flyse, fleece

Foison, A.N., abundance

Forne, A.S., before, sooner

Foone, foes

Forblowynge, A.S., blown up, swollen

Flyse, Fleece

Glede, a burning coal, a spark of fire

Gold-borned, burnished with gold

Gothe, goeth

Golden axtre, of the sun

Gree by grec, A.S., step by step

Gryside, of gryfed, A.S., grieved

Hem, very ; them ; he or him

Her }
Here } pron. their
Hir }

Heste } A.S., command, pro-
Heeste } mise

Hire, Her ; obj. case of she, is often put for herself, and without the usual preposition

Herber, A.S., lodging

Hildeforne, S. Ildefonso

Hove, A.S., to stop, or hover ; to lift ; to move, &c.

Holpe } Help, helped
Holpyn }

Hondys, A.S., hands

Hoote, A.S., hotly, eagerly

I- or y-loke, locked up

Iades, Pleiades

Iliche, alike

Iocounde, A.N., joyous, pleasant

Judicum, the Book of Judges

Jurdection } A.N., jurisdiction
Jurediction }

Kynrede, A.S., kindred

Konne } A.S., bold, boldness ;
Konnynge } to know, knowing

Lees } A.S., to gather ; to se-
Lese } lect ; to lose ; to deli-
} ver ; to lie, falsehood

Levene, A.S., lightning

Liche, A.S., like

Lifelode, A.S., living, state of life

Lere, A.S., learn

List, A.S., to please

Liggyng, A.S., lying down

Loggyng, lodging

Loughen, laughed

Lore, A.S., lost, knowledge

Male, A.N., portmanteau

Malencolye, illwill

Marce, the star Mars

Meredene, meridian

Meint, A.S., mixed

Morowe } A.S., morning, morrow
Morwe }

Me, A.S., not, nor

Nolde, A.S., would not

Nevene, A.S., to name, to speak

Oo, one, aye, ever

Ov'goon, A.S., overgo, to pass [over

Parfigt } A.N., perfect
Parfite }

Peregalle, equal

Peine, A.N., penalty, grief

Platly, A.N., flatly, plainly

Plete } A.N., to plead
Pletyth }

Plinius, Pliny the elder

Possede, possess

Pouste, A.N., power

Purviance, providence, foresight

Poyntel, a pencil for writing

Queme } A.S., to please
Quemme }

Raught, reached, snatched away

Reclinatory, a resting-place
Rede, counsel
Rewe, A.S., to pity or regret
Rewis, beams or rays
Routhe, A.S., pity, compassion
Rothir, A.S., rudder
Sapience, the Book of Wisdom
Sawter, the psalter
Scephea, Sophia
Sekeness, sickness
Sekirnesse, A.S., security, surety
Selde, seldom
Serpentyne, pertaining to the serpent
Sirquidrie } O.N., presumption, arrogance, conceit
Surquedrie }
Sith } A.S., since
Sithen }
Skylle, A.S., reason
Smerte, pain
Son, sound
Sote } sweet
Soote }
Sowkyng, sucking
Spica, a star in the left hand of Virgo
Sterre, A.S., a star
Sufferant, A.N., forbearing
Suffisaunce, sufficient
Swage, to assuage, to lessen
Tauriche, Lesser Tartary
Thilke, A.S., this same, that same
Thoo, A.S., then, when

Thoug, though
Thourg, through
Thrid, A.S., third
Thritty, A.S., thirty
To fore } A.S., before
To forn }
To fyn, A.N., to end
Tresorere, A.N., treasure
Trestisse, trusty, trusting
Trewer, A.N., truce
Triacle, a remedy, an antidote ; there was anciently a medicine of this name, which seems to be the allusion meant
Trowe, A.S., to believe, to think
Twynne, to separate, to divide
Undirpigte, A.S., propped up
Verrey, A.N., true
Waker, A.S., watcher
Wawe, woe
Wawes } A.S., seas, waves
Wawys }
Weme, A.S., corrupt
Weren, were
Werrey, to make war, worry
Worch }
Worche } to work, working
Worchynge }
Wote, A.S., to know
Ye } A.S., eye, eyes
Yen }
Yfalle, fallen
Ysage, wise